CARRIERS OF DEATH

THE DEPARTMENT Z SERIES

CARRIERS OF DEATH

DEPARTMENT Z

JOHN CREASEY

OPEN ROAD

INTEGRATED MEDIA

NEW YORK

This edition published in 2024 by Open Road Integrated Media, Inc.
180 Maiden Lane
New York, NY 10038
www.openroadmedia.com

CARRIERS OF DEATH

1

WORK FOR THE ARRANS

Their friends admitted that Timothy and Tobias, the Arran twins, were sunny-tempered folk, although Toby in particular could rid himself when the need arose of a flood of invective that was more than colourful. Both the Arrans were small, dapper men and if Tim was handsome to the point of absurdity, Toby's cheerfully ugly face was at least enlivened by a pair of fine, grey eyes. Those eyes held an expression that was not altogether pleasant as he stood, half-clad, before his dressing-table mirror, a letter in his hand.

'Women,' he was saying bitterly. 'Women! They're all the same and they always mean trouble. The Lord alone knows why He made 'em. If I had my way, I'd tell this perishing little pest just where she could go.'

Immaculately clad, as ever, Timothy perched on his brother's bed and surveyed him with what Toby always termed his owlish look.

'On the other hand,' he said slowly—where Toby spoke with the staccato abruptness of a machine-gun, Timothy always drawled— 'we can't let the old boy down. And if the poor girl—what *is* her name?'

'Smith.'

'Oh. The Derbyshire Smiths?'

Toby's voice took on a note of patient entreaty: 'Try,' he implored, waving the letter, 'to be a little less of a blithering idiot. Try—not that I think you'll succeed—to knock this one simple fact into your thick skull. Miss Smith is arriving here at three o'clock this afternoon, the time we proposed to take *Glennia* from Southampton. Try, drat you, to realise that if we wait for her, we shall miss the boat. If we miss the boat, we'll be late in New York. If we're late in New York, we shall miss Craigie—and for all we know he'll have an urgent job for us. Where's my shirt?'

'Am I your keeper? Be reasonable, Toby! It isn't the girl's fault, and we promised.'

'*You* promised,' Toby corrected acidly.

'You dirty dog,' drawled Timothy, unruffled 'You were there when I promised old Potter we'd keep an eye on her, any time he wanted, so it's your fault as much as mine.'

'You mean it doesn't matter if we miss our boat, providing she catches hers! Why can't Potter look after his own nieces, instead of letting them litter London for us to pick up?'

Timothy Arran digested this in contemplative silence, then rose slowly and walked to the door.

'There are times,' he announced, 'when you're impossible. There are other times when you're worse—and this is one of them. Catch your bally boat: I'm waiting in London for Miss Smith.'

Alone, Toby automatically selected shirt, collar and tie, and dwelt on the cussedness of fate. Normally, he admitted, he would have been glad enough to have shepherded the girl: Potter was a North Country friend of the Arran family, and his niece was travelling alone to the South of France. An old man and a cautious one, apparently, Potter was convinced that no girl of twenty-two could safely negotiate London by herself, and he had accordingly written to the Arrans asking them to look after her for the single day and night she would be spending in the capital. He had left it so late that it was impossible for the Arrans to wire or telephone regrets: Miss Smith was already on her way to London and would arrive in the early afternoon.

Toby's gloom deepened every minute. He had looked forward to the trip to New York with more zest than usual. For one thing, it was a year since his last decent sea voyage, and he was a good sailor. For another, Gordon Craigie had made one of his rare excursions away from England and Whitehall, and the Chief of Department Z had arranged to meet his two agents at the Manhattan Hotel on the fifteenth of February. It was now the ninth, and the next fast ship was to miss Craigie, who would be starting back from New York on the seventeenth. The real trouble—as Timothy might have divined had he been a little less annoyed—was that Toby really was convinced that Craigie must have found a job for them in the States. True, Craigie had maintained it was a holiday trip, pure and simple. But Toby had known Craigie for seven years and had learned most that there was to know about the man...

Some ten minutes after Tim's departure, Toby regarded himself in the mirror, delivered a satisfactory verdict, scowled and said aloud: 'Blast Miss Penelope Smith!' and left the flat. He knew that if his brother had been working—or what the Department called working—Penelope could have gone to perdition. But the voyage was to be a holiday trip—and dammit, Timothy had hinted, they could surely put their holiday off to help a friend?

'Oh well,' Toby mentally conceded, and headed for the

shipping company's office to cancel their booking for the *Glennia*. That done, he walked to the Carilon Club—and was irritated to find no one there able to offer him a game of billiards: for February, the club was remarkably empty. Taking a copy of *The Times*, he dropped into an armchair—and promptly found fault with the leading article. In fact he was so incensed by the leader-writer's views that the voice at his elbow startled him.

'A telephone call for you, Mr. Arran. From your residence, sir.'

'Oh, thank you.' Toby threw *The Times* aside, earning a glare from a retired Colonel as he cantered to the telephone in the lounge. The voice of his manservant greeted him.

'I thought I might find you at the Club, sir. I thought I should communicate with you at once. There is a cablegram from America, sir.'

'Is there, b'God,' said Tobias. 'Right, Heggson, I'll be along. Telephone around and see if you can find Mr. Timothy, will you?'

'Very good, sir.'

Toby replaced the receiver, his eyes agleam. He would be more than disappointed if the cablegram was from anyone but Craigie, and as he taxied from the Carilon Club he told himself there was no one else in America likely to send him an urgent message. Was this to be a 'come at once' summons? If so, poor Penelope would be deserted and Mr. Potter badly let down.

One glance at the somewhat childish wording was all Toby needed: the cable was from Craigie. He took it into the library and set to work on it eagerly. To a man who knew the prevailing code it was easy enough to decipher, and minutes after he had reached the flat, Toby was leaning back in his chair and smiling beatifically. There might be times, he admitted, when Penelope Smith was well on the side of the angels, for the message ran:

'RETURNING LONDON FOURTEENTH STOP MAKE ALL ENQUIRIES GREGORY MARLIN EIGHTY-EIGHT WARRITER STREET LONDON.'

If Potter and Penelope Smith had not upset the Arrans' arrangements, the twins would have been on the mid-day train to Southampton, and have known nothing of the cable until their return weeks later.

If he failed to receive an acknowledgement from the twins, Craigie would have cabled someone else—and the Arrans would have cursed till they were blue, at starting late on the job. They took a quiet pride in his confidence in them: Craigie often testified that although he had had many men working for him more capable of playing a leading part in any venture, he had never known two more doggedly and reliably ready, at any time, to walk off blindly at his nod into the death that might be waiting round the corner. Moreover, while Craigie probably lost more men through marriage than through those mysterious causes familiar to all who have read of the Department's activities, the Arrans remained single and so far unattached.

Theirs was a peculiar life. They could be said without exaggeration to have dedicated their lives to serving England in the most 'hush-hush' jobs in the world—with a cheerfulness and willingness it would have been hard to beat. They would have been embarrassed even to think of themselves as the unsung heroes they assuredly were; but subconsciously at least they would not have hesitated to apply the term to

Gordon Craigie. They knew that he had his finger on the national and the international pulse, and that there were times when danger threatened: perhaps of world-wide holocaust, perhaps of assault on Britain's mandated territories or commercial interests. They knew that when Craigie scented such a danger, he set to work and he called on them; they were the general utility men of the Department called Z or, by the pedantic, the British Intelligence.

Probably the Arrans worked as they did for the love of the game itself, for they were a pugnacious couple and did not object to the whine of bullets or other things as unpleasant. They had borne a charmed life, watching a hundred men go into the turmoil of international intrigue and die through it— men like Matthews and Carris, Bob Curtis and Righteous Dane. Splendid men, all of them, and men the Arrans had been proud to know—although they would not for the life of them have voiced that pride. They had seen others fall by marriage and scarce forborne to jeer—although Timothy Arran had once fallen very heavily in love. The girl had died; which perhaps explained a lot...

The injunction to investigate the activities of the unknown Mr. Marlin left them in no doubt: Craigie *had* found something in the States to worry him. The fact that he was returning to England ahead of schedule, and wanted a dossier on Gregory Marlin ready and waiting, meant that he expected developments on this side of the Atlantic, and the Arrans were accordingly all agog. They blessed Penelope Smith—and tossed for which of them should meet her and which make the first, tentative enquiries about Mr. Marlin.

'Heads,' Timothy offered, hopefully.

'Tails,' said Toby with great satisfaction. 'Bad luck, old boy! Tuck Penelope away safely for a few hours; I'll phone the flat as soon as I can. If I haven't called before five, I'll get through to the Eclat.'

'Go steady,' Tim warned, and Toby grinned as he headed for his bedroom.

'Do I ever do anything else?'

In tacit proof of his natural caution, he proceeded to spend a full five minutes in his selecting, from a nice assortment of major and minor weapons, of two automatic pistols and a thin knife.

He slipped the latter between his suspender and his leg: he was hardly likely to need them that day, but one never knew... Returning to the sitting-room, he bade Timothy farewell and set off to find Warriter Street, E.C.4 in a jubilant mood. The hunt was on again, and he couldn't wait to get started.

Mr. Gregory Marlin was a tall man, spindle-shanked, and unpleasantly thin. His skin was the colour of yellowish parchment, but his face was remarkably smooth: the parchment effect, oddly enough, did not make him look old. A reliable observer would have put him down as thirty-five—and been within a year or two of the mark. His hair was thick and straight, his clothes untidy and his shoes large. He looked more like a scientist or a man of letters, but was in fact one of the Stock Exchange's most astute and successful brokers— qualities not always found together.

At the time that Timothy and Toby were first discussing Penelope Smith, Gregory Marlin had been having an early lunch with two of his most important clients: Sir Miles Bradley and Charles Moran, both industrialists of international repute. The lunch was successful, for Marlin reported a profitable burst of selling, and Moran and Bradley always liked to make money. They shook hands with their broker at a minute past two-thirty and, both mellowed by sherry, returned to their own offices voting Marlin a queer customer but a damned good fellow.

Gregory Marlin was smiling to himself as he walked from the restaurant to his offices. He wondered sardonically what the others would have thought if they had known just what he was planning and just why he needed the money that came from his commissions. He had a bank balance of something over a hundred thousand pounds, and he was anxious to increase it to a million; there were ways and means, particularly to a man without scruple.

At two-fifty he entered his office. On passing through the ground floor passage of the building he had seen a small, remarkably ugly man who was gazing vacantly at the board which proclaimed the names of the people and companies who shared Number 88. Marlin was a man of varied faculties, and had noted the glance that passed between the hall-porter and the ugly man.

As he settled at his desk, he found himself wondering if the man could for some reason have bribed the porter to point him out. The unease was only momentary, however. Immersed in a welter of figures that were promising in the extreme, and filled with satisfaction at the way certain market prices were going, he soon forgot everything but money—until his telephone bell ran. Recognising the deep voice of the speaker at the other end of the wire, he frowned.

'Hello, Benson. What's worrying you?'

'I was just coming to see you, Marlin,' said his caller. 'But I passed the entrance. Have you been out to lunch?'

'Yes. I've been back twenty minutes.'

'Then you probably saw him. A little man with an ugly face?'

'Yes?' Gregory Marlin's annoyance at being interrupted changed to concern. Benson was looking after one end of the little scheme Marlin hoped to bring to a head within the next few months, and Benson was not a man to raise an unnecessary scare. 'Why?'

'Have I ever told you,' Benson parried, 'of that man Craigie?'

'Craigie? I don't—wait a minute.' Marlin's lips tightened suddenly, and his eyes narrowed. Of course. According to Benson, Craigie and his precious Department agents were likely to be the biggest stumbling block in his campaign. 'Yes, I remember. What about him?'

'Arran, outside your place, is one of Craigie's men,' said Benson softly. 'I don't like the look of that. Craigie's in America at the moment, and he may have got on to something over there. Heard from Northway lately?'

'No.' Northway was handling the American angle of Marlin's affairs and suspicion leapt into the broker's mind. 'Do you think he's been talking?'

'There's no need for him to talk if Craigie's interested in him,' Benson told him. 'Craigie has ways and means of discovering a lot of things. I wondered why he'd gone to America and I'm beginning to be afraid he's smelt something.'

'I see,' said Gregory Marlin, very softly. 'I see. But Craigie's in America, you say? And this man Arran isn't likely to discover anything by watching me. Provided you go carefully...'

'Arran and his other men,' Benson interrupted, 'have a remarkable way of getting information, Marlin, and I think you'd be well advised to put paid to him. I know—' At the other end of the line Benson was smiling to himself: there were few men in the country who knew anything about Department Z beyond the fact that it existed, and many refused to believe even that: '—that Craigie is short-handed. Since Burke left him after the O'Ray job, he's found no one to replace him. Craigie was still in America this morning, and I am assured has no plans to leave before the fourteenth. It looks as if he's leaving it to the Arrans to look after this end of the job for him. And if the Arrans were to fade out before he gets here...'

Benson broke off, but Marlin hesitated for a moment, a dozen thoughts flashing through his mind. He summarised them slowly:

'You're taking a lot for granted, Benson. Arran may have been outside by accident.'

'You can cut that idea *right* out,' Benson told him emphatically. 'Arran's watching you. Which means his brother will be in it, too.'

Marlin's thoughts raced. 'But if you do get rid of Arran,' he objected, 'you're giving the game away, man!'

'Craigie won't need telling,' Benson said grimly. 'He knows.'

'You seem very sure of yourself.'

'I watched Craigie's men working, once.' Benson laughed shortly: 'I didn't like it. Now he's scented trouble with you, he'll stick to you until he's got you—or you've got away with what you're after. And the only way you can do that is to start cutting his claws first.'

'I don't like it,' Marlin insisted. 'Granted you're right, and Craigie's dangerous. If you kill the Arrans, he'll need no more telling he's on the right track.'

'He doesn't need any more!' Benson retorted, impatient. 'Here's the position, Marlin, like it or not! Craigie's after you, and short-handed or not he'll do the damage *if* you don't make the odds too heavy against him right away. There are only five really good agents in England at the moment—as far as I know. Their names will mean nothing to you so we'll leave them. Two of those men are working on another job; the Arrans are on this. Get rid of that couple and the odds are reduced.'

'Ye-es,' Marlin scowled. 'But that means murder—and murder means the police.'

'I'll look after the police,' said Benson, 'And as for murder— you're not getting squeamish, are you? What you've got to worry about is speeding up the job. How long will it take you to get everything clear?'

'A month, at least.'

'Say, three weeks after Craigie's back? We ought to get away with it. Listen, Marlin. You want this thing to go through and it doesn't matter a damn what damage you do. But let the Arrans get properly busy, and you'll be running a risk all the time.'

Again Marlin hesitated, tapping his desk with a silver pencil. Then finally he nodded, in silent decision. He had never found the other man let him down yet—and he had good reason for his great faith in Benson's ability to cover up crimes, both minor and major.

'All right, Benson. Go ahead.'

'Good.' There was no expression in Benson's tone, and Marlin could have told from that alone that he was preparing the job in his mind, as coolly and cold-bloodedly as Marlin would have made a debtor bankrupt. 'I'm at a call-box two hundred yards from your office. I'll get a taxi right away, and meet you outside Number eighty-eight. Then I'll drop you at the club—Arran is bound to follow me afterwards. He'll feel he knows where to find you, so he'll be more interested in your friends.'

'I'll come down.' Now that he had agreed to Benson's arrangements, Marlin was prepared to leave their execution entirely in the other's hands...

Thus it happened that Toby Arran saw Marlin—whom he recognised because of the hall porter's wink—enter the taxi in which a thick-set, florid-faced man was already ensconced. Following in another, he saw Marlin enter the Junior Artists Club in Oxford Street, alone. Since the florid-faced man was the unknown quantity, Toby naturally gave his driver instructions to continue after the cab.

That he might be walking into a trap did not enter his mind. He had met ruthlessness with opponents of the Department often enough, but there was nothing in the present affair to suggest he was to meet it in a more highly concentrated fashion than ever. True, he frowned unconsciously as he saw the thick-set figure leave his taxi at Aldgate and board a bus, but he caught the same bus with little trouble and told himself the prospect seemed quite promising.

At Cambridge Road, his man alighted. Following him out, and strolling along in his wake, Toby tried to look casual. He knew his chances of shadowing the fellow unsuspected were small, now: the other must realise he was being dogged, whether his conscience was clear or otherwise. But Benson never once looked round.

The trail led through those murky quarters of the East End which the Arrans knew comparatively well—and Toby kept his right hand in his pocket, about an automatic. The further he went, the less he liked the way this was going.

They had reached the gloomy heights of a line of railway arches when the thing happened. For the first time, Benson turned round. As though he had forgotten something, he snapped his fingers in feigned irritation. The gesture took his right hand to his chest—and the lightning-like grab at the gun in his shoulder-holster beat Toby by two seconds.

Two shots, with no more sound than a whisper. Two flashes of flame. Two bullets in Toby Arran's chest...

Toby didn't even cry out. He dropped in his tracks, as the man named Benson hurried past him.

2

PENELOPE HAS A SHOCK

Penelope Smith had no particular desire to spend a holiday in the South of France. Mrs. Jeremy Potter was a dear old soul and Penelope loved her; but the prospect of four or five weeks on the Riviera with unnecessary but inevitable restrictions—or else strained relations—was not the younger woman's idea of a perfect holiday. Yet she disliked the thought of hurting the feelings of her uncle and aunt, and she had agreed to join Mrs. Potter that week-end. Jeremy himself, however, left her absolutely speechless when he declared that he had arranged for her to be in good hands for the day she would be in London; she laughed so much that she had no time to be annoyed.

'Don't you think,' she had demanded, while Jeremy regarded her with mingled sternness and amusement—his sense of humour was at least as deep-seated as his conviction that where young women were concerned Victorian ways were best—'don't you *really* think I can look after myself for twenty-four hours, Uncle Jerry? Do I really seem as helpless as all that?'

'Like all young women,' Potter twinkled, 'you are twice as helpless as you think you are. You ought to be grateful, Pen. The Arrans are a couple of nice young fellows—and I might have handed you over to Mark.'

'Heaven forbid!' Penelope Smith knew Jeremy's brother for a Victorian without a saving grace. 'Well, where am I to meet them?'

'In the foyer of the Éclat Hotel, my dear. Now hurry, or you'll miss that train.'

Jeremy himself drove her to the station, where—being what he liked to call 'in good time'—they had to wait. Thus, thoroughly bored even before the journey started, Penelope dared not think further ahead than London: the weeks at Cannes could only be dull beyond words.

She doubted whether the two young men recommended by Jeremy Potter would be very much below the forty mark. Probably they would be stiff and formal and very conscious of the weight of their responsibility for twenty-four hours. Penelope sighed. At least to have had one day in London absolutely unfettered, would have toned her up for the ordeal to follow...

She reached London soon after two o'clock. As she signed the hotel register, the clerk said:

'Oh, yes, Madam. Mr. Arran has been enquiring for you.'

Penelope, her heart in her mouth, saw him smile assurance at someone out of sight, and out of the corner of her eye, saw the someone—immaculate in medium-grey—rising from a nearby armchair. By the time she had finished signing and turned round, she had a vision of the sartorial perfection of Timothy Arran in all its glory.

'Miss Smith?' Tim's brows rose interrogatively.

Penelope stared. She had hardly dreamed of finding this absurdly good-looking young man her guardian for twenty-four hours. She liked what she saw—especially the twinkle in his grey eyes.

'Yes,' she said, 'Which one are you?'

'Timothy,' said Timothy. 'To my friends—and I'm sure you are one. Toby's gone on a crawl somewhere, but he'll roll up. Tired? Or hungry?'

'Both, really,' she admitted. 'I hate eating on the train. And the only man in the carriage let the tunnels get halfway before he pulled up the window, so I'm dirty too.'

'Never let it be said'—Timothy could be gallant when he liked—'that you can look nicer than you do!'

He grinned. 'Tell me—do you like the ordinary things? Steak, grilled and etcetera?'

'I do.'

'I had an idea you would,' Timothy approved. 'I'll order it while you get tidied—Penelope? or Penny?'

'Penelope, please!'

'Penelope it is—now, be a heroine and hurry. I waited lunch for you.'

Two things happened in the next five minutes which Timothy Arran, busy ordering steak and other things, did not know. First, Penelope Smith laughed so often in her relief that the hotel maid wondered whether she had Indulged, while on the train. The other thing was very far removed from Penelope, although it was to approach her before many hours were past.

Mr. Jacob Benson, fresh from the attack on Toby Arran at Bethnal Green, was safely away from the spot and in a telephone kiosk in the Whitechapel Road. He found the Arrans' number and put a call through. Heggson answered it, sepulchrally: No, no idea where. Mr. Timothy, Heggson understood, had gone to the Éclat hotel. Could he telephone a message?

'I'll call him myself,' said Benson.

In fact, however, he took a taxi straight to the Éclat Hotel and was in the grill-room there when Timothy and his companion entered. Smiling behind his heavy, dark moustache, Benson left. Outside, he again made use of a telephone kiosk—and before Timothy or Penelope were through their steaks, two men were watching the entrance to the hotel. Their orders were explicit, and they had every intention of carrying them out, for both men had a respect for Jacob Benson that was tantamount to fear.

Unaware of the events of the past hour, Timothy weighed into the delayed lunch—and Penelope. He found her quite remarkably attractive: none of the nervous up-from-the-country nonsense he had feared—yet nothing bored or blase, either. She had lovely teeth and laughed a lot; her eyes were hazel, her hair dark, and her complexion faultless. For the second time in his life, Timothy was really attracted: already, he wished she was to be in London for more than a day. He even regretted the cable from Craigie: the search for Gregory Marlin might need time and attention, and the thought of neglecting Penelope filled him with gloom.

'I had a fear,' she admitted, early on, 'that you would be a junior edition of Uncle Mark. Do you know him?'

'Do I know him!' Timothy echoed. He grinned engagingly, changing the subject. 'Tell me—you're not a stranger to London, are you?'

Penelope's eyes clouded suddenly.

'No... I lost my—people—four years ago. We lived here until then.'

'Oh.' Timothy mentally kicked himself. 'I'm sorry I—'

'There's no need to be. Four years is a long time.' Her smile was back again, now: 'Tell me—when am I going to meet Toby? He's late, isn't he?'

19

'Hard lines, old chap,' Tim told himself, aloud and woefully. 'I've been inspected and found wanting! But I'll tell you—he's no fellow to look after a delicate maiden. We're not on speaking terms more than once a month. I don't know,' he added judicially, 'that I should be carrying out Uncle Jeremy's wishes if I introduced you to him—'

'If he's anything like you,' Penelope put in, refreshingly, 'I'll have my hands full.'

'If he's anything like me—!' said Timothy, mock-offended. He offered cigarettes: 'Peace-pipe?'

'No, thank you,' said Penelope. 'I rarely do.'

'Another virtue,' marvelled Timothy, lighting his own. 'I can't believe it: Uncle Jeremy must have a medal for this week's good deed. Do you know,' he added, in a burst of confidence, 'that if your letter—his letter I mean—had come one hour later, Toby and I would have been on the way to Southampton and you would have been a maiden all forlorn!'

'Seriously?' she demanded.

'Yes, we'd booked for the States—no, don't go saying you're sorry! We had a cable later to tell us to stay here, so you did us two good turns.'

'I don't know that I believe you.'

'There's *one* flaw, anyhow,' Timothy teased: 'Not a trusting nature!' He smiled: 'Now if you'd like to come to the flat, Toby may be there. What ideas have you got for the night's amusement, by the way? Early dinner—and a show?—Dancing? Or an early show and a quiet evening?'

'I'll leave it to you,' said Penelope, a little dazed.

'You'll be tired to-morrow, then!' retorted Timothy.

For February, it was a warm day. The sun was shining and they elected to walk to Auveley Street, where the Arrans had their flat. Even had he been alone, it is doubtful whether Tim would have seen anything suspicious in the sudden movement of two men towards a waiting car, as he strolled with Penelope towards Bond Street.

The car followed them, driving slowly, but too far away to invite Timothy's particular notice. He did see it when they reached the North Auveley Street corner where they had to cross the road. Taking Penelope's elbow, he car-rolled: 'Beacons to the right, beacons to the left—but never a beacon in the Auveley Streets. What's that fellow going to do?'

That fellow was the small car, which had seen better days and was coming towards them. It swerved to the left, and Timothy heard its brakes give a comforting squeal.

'A driver with sense,' he said. 'I—Oh *my God!*'

He spoke and acted in one and the same moment, but in the split-second that he had for thinking, he dreaded the worst would happen. In the same split-second Penelope cried: 'All right!' and leapt forward, with the nose of the car a few feet away and the engine roaring fit to kill. As Tim sprang sideways, the wing of the off-side wheel caught his coat and sent him sprawling, face down—but he was still thinking fast, his right hand moving towards his pocket even as he rolled over. Safe on the other side of the road, Penelope stared in disbelief.

There was a little thing, glinting blue-grey, in Timothy's right hand. She saw him level it before she realised what it was. She saw the two stabs of yellow flame—but heard no sound, other than a shout from someone in the car as it swerved across the road to hit the kerb, bounced off and careered on. She heard Tim swear, even above the roar of the car's engine, when his gun jammed. Before he could fire again, the car had swung round a corner, and even a less experienced man than Timothy Arran would have realised that pursuit was useless.

Pocketing his gun, he scowled, then looked across at Penelope. His nose was smarting and as he walked slowly towards her, he touched it and looked down to see a spot of blood on his finger.

'Would you believe it?' he said, indignantly. 'They've skinned my nose!'

Timothy, for all his alleged disinterest in the female sex, was a shrewder judge than most. There would be no glossing over of the adventure, where Penelope Smith was concerned.

Dabbing at his nose with his handkerchief as he reached her he said lightly: 'Sorry about that. You all right?'

'Yes... But Tim, what *happened?* What on earth made you *shoot?*'

'Reflex action, pure and simple.' He grinned. 'Any damage?'

'No, I got clear. But you must have hurt yourself. Did you—much?'

'A bump or two and a bruise or two and the skin off my nose, drat the man! And bang goes a new suit. Taking you about is getting expensive, young lady—I'll have to send a bill to uncle.'

He smiled into her eyes, and she seemed to read the message. 'We'd better hurry or I'll get a bad reputation—torn trousers are hardly Auveley Street. It's lucky there was no one about.'

'I don't know,' said Penelope dubiously, as they turned towards his flat. 'They might have stopped the car.'

'There was just one way of stopping that car.' Timothy looked grim. 'And that was with skin and bone. You didn't notice it's number, I suppose?'

'I'm sorry. I was too—flabbergasted.'

'Fancy that,' said Timothy, with a sudden lightening of tone. 'I wonder why? Well, here we are. Our man Heggson will get worked up over this, but he'll get over it. Do you drink whisky, Penelope Smith?'

'No.'

'Good. One finger of whisky and two fingers of soda for you, my dear, while I'm changing and putting plaster on my nose. Doctor's orders. Then, because I know life won't be worth living until I've told you, I'll explain a little. Only a little, mind you.'

It was in Penelope's mind to refuse the whisky-and-soda but there were some things you could not refuse Timothy Arran, small man though he was.

He was wise also, she realised later, for the spirit warmed and steadied her. She was able to think more clearly as she waited by the fire while Heggson, who had taken the apparition of his bloodstained and dusty employer with remarkable philosophy, attended to Timothy's needs.

Well, she hadn't been dreaming. She had been walking along Auveley Street, the car had come and *deliberately* tried to run her down—or them down—and Timothy Arran had drawn an automatic from his pocket and fired after the car. She'd seen it with her own eyes. And—and Uncle Jeremy had sent her to the Arrans to make sure she came to no harm! She began to laugh and she was still laughing when Timothy appeared silently at the doorway. He scowled.

'Is there a joke?'

'Oh, Tim—I'm sorry, but I couldn't help it. I was thinking of Uncle Jeremy's face...'

'What's the matter with it?' asked Timothy, sitting down and lighting a cigarette. His eyes twinkled. 'You were worth meeting, Penelope, and I don't know how I would ever have forgiven myself if that car had done its job properly. Although,' he added, serious again, 'I suppose I would have been somewhere where forgiveness is spontaneous. It was a close one and I don't mind admitting it.'

The laughter died suddenly from Penelope's eyes, too.

'I know. I've never been so scared in my life.'

'You kept your nerve,' said Tim, 'or we'd have mixed each other up, trying to be heroes. I'll remember that. Well—I suppose you know it was a deliberate run-down?'

'I guessed. It couldn't have been anything else.'

'Well,' said Timothy soberly. 'It's a long story, and I can't tell you much, anyhow. Have you ever heard of the Special Branch, Penelope?'

She nodded, wide-eyed.

'Yes? Well, that explains the gun. I'm one of them, and I'm working on a little job—but until half an hour ago, I'd no idea what kind. I'm afraid that'll have to be enough explanation, Penelope. The only other thing I can say is that I'm glad you're due in Cannes the day after to-morrow. If I'd had to look after you for a week, in the circumstances, I'd have to put you in a padded cell.'

'But, Tim—' She eyed him mutinously, and Timothy pressed her shoulder gently.

'Please, Penelope? Not a word to a soul. And no questions—even to Toby or me?'

He smiled gravely into her eyes, and after a moment or two, she shrugged resignedly.

'Well, I don't have much option, do I? And at least,' she added, with a glimmer of a smile, 'you've given me something to think about. I've never seen a gun fired, before. It had one of those silencer things, didn't it?'

'It's fitted with a silencer, all right—' He stopped at the sudden *brrrrr* of the telephone. 'There are times,' he added, drily, 'when I wish that thing to—excuse me. Hello? Yes, Arran speaking.'

Penelope Smith had seen a great deal to surprise her since her arrival in London, but the change she saw in Timothy Arran's face as he listened to the caller astonished her. If ever a face looked like thunder, his did now.

His voice, too, had changed: suddenly, it was hard and metallic.

'Right. I'll be there in half an hour. Yes, half an hour. And get Chadwell—Sir Keith Chadwell. Damn the expense—*get Chadwell!*'

He replaced the receiver and swung round. For a second he stared at Penelope and she felt she had never seen such misery in a man's yes—nor such grimness in a man's bearing. He did not look small, now.

'Toby's been shot,' he said. 'The odds are a hundred to one against him. You'll stay here until a man named Carruthers comes—Bob Carruthers: Heggson knows him. Bob will look after you until you're on the boat, if I can't. Do just what he says—they may think you're in this thing too, and I wouldn't give tuppence for your chances if they do, should you take any risks.'

Without waiting for an answer he swung out of the room. Dazed, she watched him go, calling to Heggson as he went. Two minutes later the front door banged and she heard him hurrying down the steps.

3

SEARCH FOR MARCUS BENSON

Timothy Arran had done many things in that two minutes. He had told Heggson to telephone Scotland Yard and ask Superintendent Miller to get to the Middlesex Hospital as quickly as possible, and to explain that Toby was hurt. Heggson was then to telephone Bob Carruthers—a fairheaded, cheerful, occasionally naïve, but always willing young man—to come and take charge of the girl, and to make sure that no one but Carruthers or other well-known callers entered the flat.

Timothy's actions were automatic as he hurried to the garage and took out his Frazer Nash. He had worked so often with Toby that the thought of either of them dying seemed fantastic, although together they had been near it often enough. The one thought that filled his mind was that Toby was lying in hospital with two bullets close to his heart, and only hours to live. Two hours...

His only hope was Chadwell: the most eminent surgeon of the day, the man who came closer to working miracles than anyone else. He'd told the hospital he wanted Chadwell—who was a friend enough of the Arrans to get there if he possibly could. But...

Two hours to live...

One of the reasons Gordon Craigie had never felt he could put the Arrans, singly or jointly, in charge of a job, was that they both lacked the little extra something that makes the born leader. They had admitted it often enough, themselves. Give them a man to tell them what to do—more important, what to avoid—and they were very nearly unbeatable: working entirely on their own, their limitations were revealed. None of Craigie's best men would have been knocked so completely off-balance, whatever the excuse. Whereas Timothy certainly had been—and so went blindly to the garage and thence towards the Middlesex Hospital, never once even considering the possibility that as one effort to get him had failed, another would come.

He was in a traffic jam in Fleet Street, cursing himself for not travelling by Underground, when the attempt came with devastating suddenness.

For a moment, he had no idea where it had come from; he knew only that three bullets had pecked into the seat behind him—and that a sudden jerk of the Frazer Nash as he crept nearer the car in front had saved him from getting them through the head. Then he realised they had come from the top of a bus.

Two men fought in Timothy Arran: the Department agent and the brother of Toby. The former wanted to investigate, the latter to get on, to see Toby—of whose two hours to live, twenty minutes had already gone. He looked upwards; the bullets might have come from any one of three buses; others might come at any moment...

A sudden surge forward of the traffic forced him to release his brakes, to avoid being bumped from behind. A gap between two buses ahead of him was large enough to let him squeeze through, so he did—telling himself it was hopeless to try to find his man, anyway, as he raced onwards. He reached the hospital without further hold-up, and within minutes was standing at Toby's bedside, staring down at him as if through a mist.

Toby's face was very pale, his eyes closed. His breathing was so faint that it seemed almost non-existent. Only the house-surgeon kept Timothy going at that moment.

'Sir Keith Chadwell will be here in ten minutes,' he encouraged. 'And if anyone can pull him through, Sir Keith can.'

'I see.' Timothy's voice was strained. 'Has he been conscious at all?'

'No.'

'When will he—?'

The surgeon rested his hand on Timothy's shoulder.

'I'm sorry, Mr. Arran, but I can promise you nothing. Rest assured that everything possible will be done. You'd better come with me, for the moment—the nurses will be moving him in a few minutes, anyhow. Come along, now.'

If Timothy Arran had been told an hour before, that he would ever need talking to like a frightened child or a shock-stunned woman, he would have laughed the idea to scorn. Nonetheless, the house-surgeon handled him like that, as he led him to his office. A wise man, he found a neat whisky— and after it, Timothy managed to throw off that terrible depression: the helplessness that seemed too acute to be real.

'Well,' he said. 'Well, I suppose there's nothing I can do but wait.' He made an effort: 'Where was he found?'

'Somewhere in Bethnal Green, I think.' The surgeon was too experienced to be rattled. 'The policeman who came with him in the ambulance is still downstairs, I believe. There was a telephone call from Scotland Yard, telling him to wait.'

Timothy's eyes brightened for the first time.

'So Miller's coming! I'd like to see this chap downstairs, if I may?'

'By all means,' said the surgeon.

The policeman was sitting somewhat unhappily on a bench in the out-patients' waiting-room. He was a young man, and inexperienced enough to be startled by the order from Scotland Yard. When the little, good-looking man entered the room and made for him, he drew himself up in instinctive recognition of authority.

'Just where did you find him?' Arran demanded, his manner forcing the policeman to respond without even realising he was talking to a stranger who had offered no evidence of his identity.

'In the arches, sir, up by the Lamb. A kid came 'ollering for me. I never lost a minute—not a second, sir.'

'See anyone about?'

'Couple of men was with him, sir. I know them well—they wouldn't have done it. They never saw no one...'

Perhaps it was as well that Superintendent Horace Miller entered the waiting-room at that moment, and took charge. He was as large and as carefully-dressed as ever, and his sandy skin and moustache still looked as though they had been dusted with flour; no Miller was ever called Dusty with more justification.

He was as stolid and dependable as he looked, too; his warm handshake seemed somehow to lend Timothy strength.

'Very sorry to hear about this,' Miller said.

'It's the devil,' muttered Timothy.

'They tell me Chadwell's here,' the Superintendent added, and was rewarded by the gleam in Timothy's eyes, 'Now—care to stay, while I ask a few questions?'

The interrogation, although it yielded little, helped at least to take Tim's mind off the thing that was happening upstairs. Alone he would have tortured himself with thoughts of the surgeon's knife, so close to Toby's heart as Chadwell tried to get the bullets and yet save Toby's life.

Miller asked two or three pertinent questions and quickly realised that five minutes would make no difference, one way or the other. The local men were at the scene of the crime, photographs were being taken and the usual formal investigations were already started. He could, he decided, afford to stay here with Tim Arran until the verdict came from upstairs: he proceeded to question the constable at greater length.

Ten minutes later he and Tim knew what there was to know about the discovery of the wounded man. A barman on his way home after the mid-day opening had discovered the body—as he had thought—and sent an urchin scuttling for the nearest policeman. Two other men had arrived before the constable, and one had gone to telephone for an ambulance. No one had admitted to hearing the shot: no one remembered seeing anything unusual, or anyone strange to the neighbour-hood. Miller conceded grimly that it was a neat job—a much tidier job than shooting a man and then trying to dispose of the body. As for motive...

There was as much use worrying about motive where the Department was concerned as trying to keep the Press off a murder if once they scented it. Miller dismissed the constable, and turned to Timothy as the door closed.

'Has Craigie been busy?'

'Yes.' Timothy explained the cable, and then snapped his fingers impatiently.

'I forgot to tell you, Miller. They had a shot at me, too.'

'You *forgot* it?'

'Yes. Someone tried to run me down. God, but I wish Craigie was here!'

'You're not the only one,' Miller said bleakly. 'Who are you after? Anyone you know?'

'A man named Marlin. Lives—or works—at eighty-eight Warritter Street. You might get busy there, Miller,' Timothy was on his toes; the possibility of making progress had cheered him more than anything else could have done; his mind was beginning to function properly again. Toby was at Warriter Street this afternoon, to watch Marlin. Probably he found something, and—oh, *damn!* What the devil's the use of probably, probably, probably...'

'Steady, old man,' said Superintendent Miller.

Arran stared at him for a moment, and then smiled, sheepishly, and without humour.

'Sorry,' he said, 'but I feel like nothing on earth. I wish to heaven the doctors would hurry up.'

'They won't be long.' Miller glanced at his watch. It was twenty minutes since the operation had started.

'When's Craigie due back?'

'On the fourteenth. I...'

The door opened and Timothy swung round like a jack-in-the-box. The smile on the house-surgeon's face was not enough reassurance for him.

'Well?' he snapped.

'Successful, we think,' said the other. 'Sir Keith's waiting to see you, Mr. Arran.'

Tim was out of the door in a flash, and the surgeon and Miller smiled at each other as they hurried after him.

The specialist was still in his surgical gown as he greeted Timothy—and if he still could not guarantee the result, he was obviously hopeful.

'We've got the bullets,' he explained, 'and with a little luck, he'll pull through. No worrying him with questions if he recovers consciousness, though.' The last words were for the benefit of Miller, whom Chadwell knew slightly. 'He might be able to talk in forty-eight hours, but not before.'

'I'll have a man near him,' Miller said. 'But he won't be worried, Sir Keith.'

'There'll be a hell of a lot of trouble if he is,' snapped Timothy. 'Can I see him?'

'Yes—for a minute or two.'

By the time Timothy returned from the private ward where Toby lay, he had recovered sufficiently to apologise to Miller for his earlier brusqueness, and to thank the surgeon gratefully. Then, satisfied that there was now more than a fifty-fifty chance, and assured that the hospital authorities would communicate with him every hour and as often as he cared to telephone, he left with Miller.

'These arches, first?' he asked, 'Or Marlin?'

'Marlin, I think.' Miller spoke gruffly, shooting a quick glance at the small man. 'But I'm not sure you ought to come, Arran.'

Timothy grinned as he pressed the self-starter of the Frazer Nash. 'Would you tell Craigie he couldn't come? This is official, Horace, and don't you forget it.'

'I won't. But listen, old man. If you really think this fellow Marlin is in it anywhere, it's not wise for you to see him. You'll be losing your temper...

'Not me,' said Tim with an assurance that revealed the depth of his faith in Sir Keith Chadwell's skill. 'No more arguing, Horace—or you can walk!'

In the event, Timothy kept his temper admirably—much as he disliked Gregory Marlin, and instinctively certain as he was that the stockbroker knew something of the shooting. Neither he nor Miller, however, had forced even a hint out of the man, and they left his office convinced that they were up against a stiff job and a tough customer.

On the face of it, so much was obvious. Within three hours of receiving the cable from Craigie, three attempts had been made on Arran lives, and each attempt had been unpleasantly close. Tim was prepared now for further trouble at any moment and he was relieved when he reached his flat to find Penelope safe and sound with Bob Carruthers.

They both jumped up as he opened the door and both fired the single question:

'How is he?'

'I think he'll pull through.' Tim grinned lopsided reassurance as they eyed him closely: he had no idea how startled they were by his pallor and obvious weariness. 'Chadwell's managed to get the bullets out. Any trouble here, Bob?'

'Not a sign.' Carruthers smiled wryly: 'Apart from Miss Smith.'

Timothy raised a questioning eyebrow at Penelope. 'Being awkward, eh?'

'Obstreperous is the word,' Carruthers corrected, cheerfully. 'Wanted to come to the hospital, and was annoyed with me when I threatened forcible restraint.' He shook his mane of blond hair in mock sorrow. 'These women—oh, these women!'

Heggson chose that moment to bring tea, and not even Carruthers could continue to paint Penelope Smith as obstreperous as she presided demurely over the large silver tray. And before tea was finished, she was introduced to two more young men; one a tall, languid and remarkably lazy gentleman by the name of Wally Davidson, and the other broader-shouldered but equally lofty, by the name of 'Dodo' Trale.

33

'Dodo,' Davidson explained, 'because he ought to be dead.'

Penelope marvelled at the cheerfulness of these men, Timothy included. There was clearly real trouble in the offing and clearly any or all of them might run into danger, just as the Arrans had done. Yet here they were, ragging each other with lazy good humour.

'The thing is,' Timothy said, serious now, 'there's just a chance that Penelope, through being with me, might meet trouble. Thank the Lord she's going to Cannes! Bob, will you look after her until tomorrow—see her on to the boat?'

Carruthers beamed.

'Will I not!'

'You will not,' said Penelope, with equal emphasis. 'It's nonsense to say I'm in danger, and—' she glanced at Timothy —'You're going to be busy, aren't you?'

'I'm going to make someone else busy,' Tim corrected grimly.

'Well, you're not going to waste time with me,' Penelope told them all firmly. 'If it will make you happier, Tim, I'll stay at the Éclat until I leave to catch the train from Victoria.'

Timothy hesitated a moment.

'You mean it?'

'Of course I do.'

'All right, then' he conceded, with something suspiciously like a sigh of relief. 'I'll let you go.'

Miss Penelope Smith left the Arran flat twenty minutes later, convinced that she was thereby cutting herself off completely from something she would have given the world to have seen to the end. She did not dream that Dodo Trale was behind her, that he stayed at the Éclat in a room in the same corridor as her own, and that he followed her to the boat next morning and watched it out of sight.

About the time she stepped on board, Timothy Arran and

Superintendent Miller reached the Middlesex Hospital. Timothy was a different man, that morning. Toby, incredibly, was progressing well and would almost certainly pull through.

It was a pale Toby who smiled wearily up at them when they reached the ward, and his voice was little above a whisper. A few minutes passed before Miller asked casually.

'Remember anything, Toby?'

Toby turned his head slowly to meet the Super's gaze. His eyes were tired, but they held a gleam.

'See Marlin,' he said. 'Another fellow—who shot me. About five-ten—very dark—red-faced. Bushy moustache. Was in a cab with Marlin.'

Exhausted by the effort, he closed his eyes. The nurse stepped forward, frowning and shaking her head. Timothy pressed his brother's hand for a moment, then followed Miller out. As the door closed, Miller's eyes were shining.

'That's tied it on to Marlin,' he rumbled. 'Another talk with that gentleman won't do us any harm, and the sooner the better. Coming?'

They saw Gregory Marlin forty minutes later. Miller did not beat about the bush. He answered the suave and sardonic inquiries of the stockbroker with a question;

'You were in a taxi with another man yesterday afternoon, Mr. Marlin. I'd like all the information you can give me about him, if you please.'

Timothy Arran, holding a watching brief, saw Martin's eyes narrow and sensed that he had had a shock; but there was no alteration in the even voice with its faintly guttural accent, nor any sudden colour in the odd, parchment-like skin.

'And what man was this, Superintendent?' Marlin smiled, and Timothy saw his teeth for the first time; they were small and very sharp, almost as if they had been filed. 'I was in several taxis with several men, yesterday.'

'Can I have their names and addresses, Mr. Maria?' Miller replied, politely and with deceptive calm. He waited, pencil poised.

'My dear Superintendent, my clients...'

Miller drew a deep breath; he could use the heavy hand when he chose, and long practice had taught him how to time the use of it.

'Come, Mr. Marlin. I don't want to be unpleasant, but this seems seriously like deliberate evasion. I'm making inquiries on a serious case and I want all the help you can give me. One of your clients...' Miller pushed his head forward an inch as he went on... 'probably shot Mr. Tobias Arran yesterday afternoon, and the consequences will probably be fatal. Mr. Arran was working for our Special Department, as I told you yesterday. The law is no thing to trifle with, as I am sure you know.'

Marlin gave way so quickly that Timothy was suspicious, but for the rest of the interview the stockbroker appeared to offer all the help he could. He submitted a list of names and addresses of people with whom he had been on the previous afternoon, and wished the Superintendent every success. Miller, glancing down the list, did not like the look of it; there were several distinguished names and he needed no more telling that Marlin was a man of considerable reputation. But for Toby Arran's muttered words, he would have told himself that suspicion of Marlin was not justified.

He would have thought differently if he could have heard Marlin talking to Jacob Benson on the telephone twenty minutes later, but in all likelihood he would have smiled dourly and told Timothy that thieves always fall out. For Marlin did not mince words.

'Miller's after you,' he snapped. 'And he's traced my connection with the shooting. My God, Benson, if you've let them get at me. I'll smash you!'

'They can't get at you,' retorted Benson. 'If anyone's got a grouch, it's me. I...'

'You started this,' Marlin warned, 'and you'll finish it on your own. I've not given your name—yet.'

There was a moment's pause; Marlin was smiling unpleasantly: this was the kind of blackmail that gave him exquisite pleasure. Benson broke the silence at last.

'I see. So if I don't lead them off, you'll shop me, will you? And what when I've talked?'

'I'm not likely to give your name,' said Marlin, very slowly, 'while you're alive. I have an idea I have overestimated your powers, my friend.'

He didn't hear Benson's reply, for he hung up. For five minutes he leaned back in his chair and closed his eyes. When he had needed work of a certain nature done, he had always employed Benson and Benson's men. He was beginning to think Benson's period of usefulness was over, and that the men would take orders from one leader as readily as another.

'Yes,' murmured Gregory Marlin to himself, 'I think that's it.' He stood up and reached for his hat, and his smile was a long way from pleasant. 'This is a lot too big for Benson to bungle. And if that man Arran is a fair specimen of Craigie's men, there isn't much trouble coming from that quarter.'

'That man Arran' was in his Auveley Street flat some thirty minutes later, opening a second cable from Gordon Craigie. He decoded it rapidly—and smiled more widely than at any time since Toby had been shot.

For the message read:

'FLYING BACK ARRIVING MIDNIGHT TO-MORROW TENTH.'

37

4

CAUSE FOR CONCERN

Gordon Graigie had not told the truth to the Arrans
when he had left England for the States. He had
guessed their anxiety to be up and doing would keep them in a
ferment while he was away, and he was anxious that they
should be at their best when eventually the need for action
arrived. At that time Craigie's agents were—as Benson had
discovered—low in numbers and possessed of no outstanding
member, and Craigie was particularly anxious to use his
forces to the best of their ability. He sighed for a man to
replace Jim Burke, who had been married six months earlier,
but knew he was not likely to find one before this job was
finished.

The 'job' was no more than a whisper when he had left for
America. In three weeks there, it had developed into a bellow
that even a dubious American Intelligence Bureau could not
ignore. Not that the Americans were less perceptive than
Craigie: it was simply that to them, the thing was incredible.

It had started three years before—three years meant little
to Department Z—when H.M.S. *Drune,* one of the new battle-

cruisers, had been damaged while in dock after her first long trial. It had been followed by a series of major and minor sabotage efforts, some of which had been successful and some frustrated—the latter usually by accident. For seven or eight weeks, in fact, a section of the British Press had been thundering warnings of a Communist threat, and even those who had never considered Communism could become a menace to this island, had begun to get worried. After the *Drune* trouble, the engines of three smaller vessels had been damaged extensively: two attempts to cause explosions at munitions factories had been only partly prevented: one fire at a War Department petrol store had destroyed five thousand gallons of oil, killed three men and injured a dozen. That was not all. Attempts, most of them fruitless, to break into Government experimental air stations had been made, and two of the latest model troop-carrying aircraft had crashed without explanation during trial flights, incurring the loss of several men. Deviously and persistently the sabotage continued.

If every incident had found its way into the press the war scare would have become even greater than it was. The Government might quieten the demands for interference in the Italo-Abyssinian struggle and the internal massacre in Spain; it could try to subdue the Palestine riots by shipping a few thousand reservists, and gain the approbation of most of the press and a goodly portion of the public, but it could not have convinced a very perturbed nation that there was nothing sinister in the sabotage and the attempts to do serious damage to sections of every branch of the fighting forces.

Perhaps only Craigie and half a dozen Cabinet Ministers, with the inevitable permanent staff, knew the real gravity of the situation. Naturally, Craigie had been asked to get to the bottom of it; as naturally he was attempting to do so.

He had still been trying to sort the wheat from the chaff

when he heard of the *Akren* catastrophe. America's finest and newest battleship—three months from the shipyard, and internationally acknowledged to be the biggest and most impregnable vessel on the Seven Seas, viewed by the Americans as a challenge and a warning to those European countries snarling at each other's throats to keep their side of the Atlantic—sank with all hands in something under ten minutes. The crews of a dozen smaller craft, part of the flotilla escorting the triumphant battleship on her maiden voyage, first saw the billowing clouds and the tongues of yellow flame, then heard the dreadful detonation—and stared, helpless and dumbfounded, as the juggernaut of the seas went down.

Remarkably, only the German and Italian press blamed the affair on to the 'Red' menace. Every other country's newspapers put it down to an accident due to a fault in the *Akren's* boilers. The world was in no state for a story of sabotage on so grand a scale—in fact, a virtual act of war—to fly on the wings of rumour, and even the more excitable Press saw the wisdom of doing nothing to inflame public opinion. But the Governments of the world were ready and waiting. The armaments race increased and the tension in High Circles was greater, perhaps, than at any time since the early days of August 1914.

So Gordon Craigie had gone to America.

There he found that, almost to a man, the authorities preferred to view the catastrophe as an accident. He met a very few who subscribed to his opinion that some country—it was far too early to say which—had deliberately wrecked the *Akren,* and as deliberately had damaged Government factories and machines in both England and America.

A myriad of inquiries had been set on foot. Craigie admitted the American Intelligence Bureau had reduced investigation to a fine art, but considered it owed a great deal to chance. And, this time, the chance was presented—as so often happened—through a woman.

Her name was Rampaz. She was young, more than usually good to look upon, soft-voiced and well-dressed. She went to Police Headquarters in New York, composed enough but anxious and worried. Her husband had been missing for five weeks; the last time she had seen him he had said he was going to smuggle himself on board the *Akren*. She had not believed it possible, but as he was still missing she was beginning to fear it had happened. Could the police give her any information?

Craigie and three other men saw her. They learned that Jake Rampaz was a journalist of reputed Communist leanings, although his wife assured them it was all talk; he was the kindest soul alive, her Jake—if he was alive. She caught her breath in shocked awareness when she added that, and Craigie felt really sorry for her. But she was their first real lead: the questioning had to go on. Among the things she told them was that Rampaz had been a close friend of a certain Julian Northway, who operated on Wall Street. And Rampaz had come home from seeing Northway the day he had boasted he would stow away aboard the *Akren*...

There are methods of interrogation in America that do not bear talking about. Although Craigie admitted they were justified up to a point—and knew that his own agents had, unofficially, resorted to similar measures in emergencies, he did not like them. Still, he took care to be present every time Northway—a naturalised American who had been born in England—was interrogated. He saw the man age from thirty-five to fifty-five in a week. He saw him a physical wreck, prostrate with exhaustion before he made any admission.

Yes, yes, he had bribed Rampaz to get aboard—they would find the papers in a small office at Manhattan Buildings. If they would only let him *sleep*... God, he must sleep! He hadn't slept for two hundred hours...

They found the papers and proved the admission true. They discovered that Rampaz—and also crew members of acknowledged Communist tendencies—had been aboard the *Akren* on the ill-fated voyage. They discovered a list of names and addresses of people in all countries, and among them was that of Gregory Marlin, of 88 Warriter Street, London, E.C.4...

But although the interrogation of Julian Northway was exhaustive, he would not admit the list of names and addresses to be anything more than a record of brokers in various capitals. Gordon Craigie and the others admitted that Northway was, if nothing else, a very brave man.

Every man mentioned on the list *was* a stock-and-share broker, but every name had been communicated to the proper quarters in the various capitals, for urgent investigation. So that when Horace Miller had taken it upon himself to report the Arran shooting to the Home Office, the Home Office had radio-telephoned Craigie at once.

Craigie was in New York when the call came. After giving certain instructions concerning Gregory Marlin, he replaced the receiver thoughtfully, then glanced across the room at the big man who sat there: Thomas Lander, Governor of New York.

'I want to fly back to England,' he told him, 'can you recommend a pilot?'

'You're serious?' Lander rumbled.

Craigie nodded, and Lander said reflectively: 'Well, you know Bob Kerr's still in town?'

Kerr's flight from England a month before had been a nine days' wonder, easily breaking the west-to-east time record. But his effort to repeat the triumph on the return flight had failed when *Wishing Bone*, his three-engined monoplane, developed a technical fault.

'I'm told he's hoping to get off in a day or two,' Lander volunteered, 'Like me to bring him here?'

'If you wouldn't mind?' Craigie said, gratefully.

An hour later, Lander was introducing him to the man whose face was already thoroughly familiar to him from newspaper photographs. There was a ruggedness about Robert McMillan Kerr's features that Craigie liked, and he warmed to the man as he felt the firm handshake and met the calm, grey eyes.

Craigie had been described by Lander as a personal friend, anxious for business reasons to return to London in a hurry, and he asked: 'Is it possible to get back tomorrow night?'

'No,' said Kerr bluntly. 'That would mean leaving by midnight tonight, at the latest, and the wind isn't likely to change. Rough over the Atlantic, and thunder going round. No chance at all, Mr. Craigie. Sorry.'

'What would be the earliest?'

'I don't know. Perhaps two days; perhaps two weeks.'

'I see.' Craigie hesitated, then asked: 'I suppose nothing would induce you to change your mind? Money is no object.'

'I don't take risks for money,' Kerr said flatly.

'You *have* taken plenty, in your time.'

'When it's suited me,' Kerr retorted. Then as Craigie

grinned quick appreciation, he smiled as if suddenly recognising a kindred spirit in the shrewd-eyed older man.

'Now I wonder,' Craigie hazarded, 'if you'd be more interested if I told you this was Government business?'

There was a change of expression in Kerr's eyes.

'Which Government?'

'At the moment, mainly Britain's.'

'Is that all you can tell me?'

'Yes,' said Craigie, 'apart from the fact that if you won't take me, I'll have to find someone who will. I must be in England, if it's humanly possible, to-morrow night. It is not...' Craigie smiled—'a matter of money; although as I said, money is no object.'

'Well, now.' Kerr paused to light a cigarette: 'I can't promise to get you to England. I've been through worse blows than there are at the moment, but of course we don't know what we'll meet halfway across. Bit of a risk.'

For an understatement, that was very close to the limit, and Craigie smiled at Lander's rumbling chuckle as he told Kerr drily: 'Well, if you'll take it, I will. Your machine is ready, isn't it?'

'It only needs fuelling. What time do you want to get to London?'

'About midnight or earlier.'

'Call it midnight or never!' said Bob Kerr. He stood up and extended his hand. 'I'll have to hurry, Mr. Craigie, to get ship-shape in time. It's at the Brooklyn field, and we can set off as soon after ten as you like.'

As easily as that, the association between Craigie and Kerr began. Neither of them knew how long it was going to last or where it was going to end, and neither of them cared. The first job was to get to England.

* * *

The London morning papers printed a stop-press to say that Robert Kerr, the famous long-distance flier, was starting his return flight in the *Wishing Bone* that day, possibly with a passenger. The evening papers had news of the flight sprawled across their front pages, with plenty of recent photographs of Kerr but none of his passenger, now named as 'Arthur Strong, an American financier.' The press were too delighted with their national hero to care about the publicity-shy Mr. Strong: the flight had been accomplished in a record sixteen-and-a-half hours and the landing at Heston had been perfect.

At ten-thirty, Craigie and Kerr climbed into a closed saloon car and were driven to London.

Both were silent, for the first few minutes, Craigie reliving the incredible experience of that flight. He knew he would remember all his life the appalling darkness, the buffeting they had endured a hundred times, the mountainous waves they had seen during the first hours of daylight, when they had been forced perilously close to the surface of the sea.

From time to time, Kerr had remarked that it was 'a bit rough', and invariably Craigie had responded: 'Making good time, aren't we?' And Kerr would nod approval, and press calmly on...

They were on the Great West Road, when Kerr spoke. He was smoking a pipe, and Craigie was wishing for his beloved meerschaum, tucked away in the single suitcase he had brought with him.

'Darned sight safer up there,' Kerr gestured skywards with his pipe, 'than on the roads. Enjoy the flight?'

45

'I did not,' said Craigie simply. 'I didn't think we'd make it.'

Kerr chuckled.

'It's no fun if you're not used to it and it's a damned bore when you are. I like the air,' he added, 'but there's a time to finish. You can tempt fate too long. I think I'll drop it. For a bit, anyhow.'

Craigie nodded thoughtfully.

'Have you anything else in mind?'

'No. I could do with a rest, anyhow.'

'Particularly anxious to have one?'

Kerr regarded him reflectively. In the dim light of the car interior, Craigie's face looked singularly gaunt and almost bleak, yet there was an air of such completely assured authority about him that Kerr, intrigued despite himself, found himself saying a cautious: 'Well—it depends.'

'I might be able to put a proposition to you, Kerr,' said Craigie, 'that would be worse than the flight. More dangerous.'

'How, more dangerous?'

'There wouldn't be so much chance of getting away with it,' Craigie told him quietly. 'You might, but you'd be up against trouble nearly all the time. Most men—' Craigie often took big decisions quickly, and he was prepared to say enough, now, to let Kerr guess what the job was—'have lasted less than a year when they've been in the thick of it. Some have managed to get away all right. But the best men don't last long.'

'Hmm.' Kerr drew at his pipe in silence for a good thirty seconds, then: 'It sounds unpleasant. Is it in England?'

'Sometimes.'

'Hmm,' Kerr repeated. 'All right. I'll think it over. If you want me, let me know.'

'If you come into it you'll have a deuce of a job to get out,' Craigie warned.

'There are times when I've been in the *Bone*,' said Kerr with a rare smile, 'and never expected to get out at all. Unofficial service work, I take it?' he added, seeing Craigie did not want to take the tacitly offered chance of dropping the subject for the time being.

'Yes.'

'What's the trouble at the moment?'

'Remember the *Akren*?' Craigie asked quietly.

The man he had met less than twenty-four hours before, nodded and looked straight ahead, thinking slowly and coolly. This was a very different development from what Kerr had expected, but he liked the sound of it. The crashing of the two troop-carriers had always appeared to him to be a great deal more than accidental. He had never heard of Craigie by name, but he knew of the existence of an Intelligence Department, and could put two and two together.

'You think it was sabotage?' he asked, and Craigie's early good impression strengthened.

'I'm sure of it. So were a lot of other things.'

'I've wondered. Any idea who's behind it?'

'Ideas, yes, but nothing else.'

'Russia, on the surface, of course?'

'Of course,' admitted Craigie. 'But you know, we need two things in mind, right now. Communism on one side Fascism on the other.'

'And nothing to choose between them,' Kerr opined.

'I don't know. We haven't seen enough of either of them, yet.' Craigie knew his remark would have shocked anyone of confirmed political views, but he had no objection to shocking people. This may be commercial, for all we know.'

Kerr allowed himself another rare smile.

The merchants of death, eh?'

'Well,' said Craigie, 'I've met some queer things in the past few years, Kerr, and that title's not inappropriate at times.

This job isn't fixed, you know. It might be one of a dozen things, and there's just a possibility that there are more genuine accidents than I like to admit.'

'Not much of a possibility,' said Kerr. 'At least I don't think so. I hope you don't want to harness me straight away? I'm dog tired. Could hardly keep awake the last couple of hours over, and did I wish you could handle the controls?'

Craigie smiled.

'It's probably as well I couldn't. No, there's no hurry to-night. But to-morrow, if you'll come and see me? Third door along Great Scotland Yard, off Whitehall. Ring three times and I'll open for you. Oh—better give me an address, in case there's anything urgent.'

'If you don't allow me a full eight hours sleep,' Kerr replied, yawning hugely, 'I'll drop out.' He yawned again. 'Sorry! I'll stay at the Flying Club, Piccadilly, to-night, and see you to-morrow. Any particular time?'

'No,' said Gordon Craigie. 'Suit yourself—but make it as early as you can.'

'Don't you ever sleep?' Kerr demanded, and Craigie laughed at what had become a time-honoured question.

'Occasionally,' he said now. 'When there's nothing else to do. I suppose you keep something to shoot with?'

'Plenty,' Kerr assured him. 'Large or small?'

'Small but fast. You'll probably need it. It will be a shame,' Craigie added, as the car drew up at the Flying Club and Kerr started to get out, 'if this thing doesn't explode, Kerr. You'll get prepared for nothing.'

'I've a queer idea,' said Robert Kerr, 'that if this misfires you'll find something else. I...'

The 'I' was as far as he got just then. He heard but did not see the car coming along Piccadilly, for he was on the blind side. But he heard and understood the things pecking into the side of the car, and he ducked automatically, while Craigie slid abruptly to the floor. For a moment the darkness of Piccadilly was split by the yellow flashes from the machine-gun that had blazed into action, and a hundred people or more stood and stared in stupefaction.

5

SEVERAL QUEER THINGS

I f Gordon Craigie had entertained the slightest doubt as to the ability of Kerr to act and think quickly, it must have disappeared in the next sixty seconds. The firing had hardly stopped as the attacking car passed out of range, before Kerr was on his feet and tugging at the arm of the saloon driver, who still sat like a waxed figure, too terrified to think.

'Slide out, damn you!'

As the man slid out, jerked into action by the bellowed command, Kerr jumped into the driving-seat, pressed the self-starter and raced the engine cruelly. Then, ignoring the cries of pedestrians and the whistles of police, he swung the saloon round on two wheels and shot off in pursuit.

The far side of Piccadilly was comparatively free of traffic; only one red light glowed—that of the car which had carried the gunmen. It was travelling at sixty but the saloon touched sixty-five and rocketed towards its object, its engine wailing like a siren. At the roundabout by the hospital, the green lights were showing and Kerr saw his quarry swing left, towards

Victoria. He followed, blessing the clear road as he drew nearer.

Craigie, unarmed, could only sit on the floor and hope for the best. He knew the machine-gun might start again at any moment, for the gunmen would not lightly give in without a fight. There was another way death could come, too; there would be a crash all too soon. This mad chase couldn't last long in London, with the late theatre crowds likely to swarm the streets at any moment. He thought of his talk with Sob Kerr and smiled grimly; Kerr was going to prove a safe bet—if he lived through this.

Robert McMillan Kerr, bending low at the wheel of the saloon, was wondering when the next shots would come. He realised this was the nearest thing to suicide he could imagine: the Atlantic flight had been child's play, in comparison. But he had never been shot at in cold blood before and didn't propose to let the gunmen get away with it. His jaw was set, and his eyes were very narrow. He didn't take them off the red light of the car in front—a Daimler—as the distance lessened from a hundred yards to fifty.

To forty... thirty...

Kerr didn't know the speed limit of the car he was driving, but it was a Talbot and likely to do well. He waited a fraction of a second longer, saw the first streak of flame from the machine gun poking from the rear window of the first car, and trod hard on the accelerator. The Talbot literally lurched forward and he swung the wheel, making for an off-side pass. He heard the bullets pecking into the radiator and the wings; two passed close to his head and through the glass, and he hoped Craigie was keeping low. It was the one thought in his mind, apart from his determination to crash the Daimler.

Headlights loomed in front of him but he ignored them.

Traffic from the other direction swerved to the pavement, while drivers and passers-by bellowing curses at the madmen, and the deadly *tap-tap-tap* of the machine-gun was drowned in the bedlam.

Twenty yards... ten...

The Talbot was well over, now, and out of range from that rear window. Kerr knew the men would swing the gun to the side, but there was just a chance he could beat them to it. He forced the nose of his own car forward until it was inches ahead of the luggage grid of the other. A foot ahead... two...

He could see the men in the Daimler now—and even the gun, less than five feet from his head. He was grimly conscious that he was very close to the end; but at least the others would not get away now. He saw the machine-gun suddenly poked towards him, and on the same instant he swung the Talbot's nose hard left, into the side of the Daimler.

The noise of the crash was incredible. The Talbot's nose smashed through the Daimler and Kerr actually saw its driver crushed into eternity. He felt his own car shiver as the other heeled over, and wondered fleetingly whether he would see the light of day again. As the Daimler's off-side reared up, its running-board locked with the Talbot's, heaving it upwards.

Craigie crashed against the roof as Kerr grabbed the near-side door-handle. For a moment, the Talbot hung in the air; then it suddenly lurched over and crashed on its side. As it settled down, Kerr was clinging to the topmost door like a fly to the ceiling.

It wasn't until the red glow came, that he knew the Daimler had caught fire.

* * *

'An auspicious start,' said Gordon Craigie some twelve hours later, 'and I'm glad you were with me, Kerr. But for the love of heaven, don't do things like that again. You deserve to be dead.'

Bob Kerr rubbed the one square inch of his chin not covered with sticking-plaster, and eyed the bandage round Craigie's head. There was another bandage beneath Craigie's coat sleeve and various patches of plaster about both their persons. But if they had not come through unscathed, they could at least be grateful things had been no worse.

'It was a bit abrupt,' admitted Kerr, with typical understatement. 'Pity the car caught fire. Everything destroyed, I suppose?'

'Everything. There were three men in it, poor devils.'

'They got exactly what they deserved.' Kerr's chin thrust a little forward. 'They had time enough to give up if they chose, and they had all the odds with them. If that fellow hadn't been a bit slow with his gun, we wouldn't be here.'

Craigie nodded. 'All the same, you mustn't take chances like that again.'

Kerr frowned.

'You wanted to get them, didn't you?'

'I didn't particularly want to lose you, or to go out myself. If we'd been nearer the end of the chase, if we'd known who was in the car and could have been sure once they were dead the thing was finished, we could have taken all the risks you liked. But they were paid men, probably. You see what I mean?'

Kerr rubbed the patch of chin again and smiled ruefully.

'Yes. Sorry, Craigie; I didn't think of that.'

The older man returned his smile. 'I have no doubt you will, another time. For the moment—well,' Craigie reached for his meerschaum and stuffed the ample bowl: 'you don't need much more telling what we're up against. Now—I've seen one or two of my other agents this morning, and I've heard what's happened over here. Ready?'

'Carry on,' said Kerr.

Craigie related the story he had heard from Timothy Arran and Horace Miller, cutting it as short as he could without omitting relevant details. Kerr nodded from time to time but did not interrupt. He was silent for a few minutes when Craigie had finished, and the Chief of Z was irresistibly reminded of Jim Burke.

Burke had been a bigger man, physically, than Kerr, although Kerr's shoulders were probably wider. But it was not so much physical resemblance as similarity of manner. Craigie had often watched Jim Burke sitting where Kerr sat now, silently chewing everything over in the same way before committing himself to an opinion. Burke had been in all the biggest Department operations until this one, and Craigie knew that had he been single, he would have given his soul to be in Kerr's place now. But Burke had married and was happy.

Craigie kept the 'no married men' rule absolutely inviolate, less from concern for the woman than from the fact that no married man worth his salt could be devoted wholly and entirely to the Department. Even 'Z' agents were human, although Craigie did his best to cancel the human element when his men were working. They were cyphers, because they had to be: he could not afford to use any man who might instinctively save himself for another's sake, when danger threatened.

The Department had to be run like that, or it would have been useless. His men won, or they died: there was no other choice. Craigie knew that the time might come when the Department would lose, despite the immensity of its organisation, and he dreaded to think of the consequences. The matters at stake were vital to the nation; the cogs in the wheel could be, and had to be, replaced.

Craigie hated the fact, but knew this attitude to be essential, and he never accepted a man to work for him until it had been made crystal clear.

There were times, of course, when 'Z's' work was confined to minor jobs which carried little danger, but when the necessity arose the Department threw in all its resources. Perhaps once, perhaps twice a year there was an upheaval that would, if all of it had reached the ears of the public, have added considerably to the scares of war and worse.

It was indicative of the state of things that there were men —in hundreds, too—prepared to take as many risks as the Department men, but for a different cause. Those who paid for gunmen offered a high reward, and the worst that could happen to a man who defied the law and society at large for money, was death, either in action or from the end of a rope. Craigie had learned only too well that there was no limit too high for the men who wanted money or power.

He couldn't be sure, yet, what turn this present job would take. The ruthlessness of it suggested the stakes were high. But it was useless to theorise too much; the task was to get Marlin and whoever was helping him.

If there had been any doubt that Marlin was behind the shooting, it had been removed late the previous day. Marlin had realised that the odds were too heavy for him to risk staying and working as usual, but a police patrol had allowed him to slip through their fingers, and it was an effort for Craigie not to feel bitter about it.

Kerr broke his silence at last, and Craigie wondered whether their thoughts had been running along familiar lines.

'This man Marlin,' Kerr said, 'could tell us a lot. In fact, he's already told us a lot.'

'How?' asked Craigie.

'By dodging off. He's backing the attacks and he's scared. The job is to get him again.'

'Yes...' said Craigie slowly. 'There's something worse than that, though. Marlin was a stockbroker, and he numbers a hundred big men among his clients. Any one of them might be financing him, and Marlin may have disappeared to make sure he wasn't detained and questioned about the others. In short, Marlin may be merely a figurehead.'

'You mean the list of suspects is a hundred strong?'

'I wouldn't go as far as that. Possible suspects only; but of course, we'll have to consider each one.'

'Hm,' grunted Kerr. 'That's nearly as long a job as waiting to see if there are any more sabotage attempts. What do you think will happen? Will we have to wait for something, or will it come to us?'

'If we don't pick up Marlin's trail,' Craigie told him, 'I think we'll have to wait for it. But it's too early to be sure, yet. The only safe thing we can say is that there are—or have been—serious attempts to damage armament factories, aeroplanes, ships and big guns. We don't know any more than that, and we've got to find out who's backing it.'

'I see.' Kerr was silent for a moment, sitting forward with his hands clasped on his knee. 'Yes. But a thought, Craigie. Not likely, of course, but a possibility, eh? Er—there are fanatics who'll go to any lengths to destroy arms. Peace at any price. No?'

For a full sixty seconds, Gordon Craigie stared at him, his first faint smile growing deeper. Then: 'You've stolen a march on me there,' he said, 'yes, it *is* possible, but I hope to heaven you haven't struck the truth.'

'Why?' demanded Kerr.

'Try to imagine anyone more difficult to get at than the fanatic,' Craigie invited. 'No direct motive, no real method—but it's absurd. The maddest peace-at-any-price fanatic wouldn't use machine-guns and the rest of it.'

'They'd be employing someone,' Kerr reasoned. 'And in this case, they seem to be using American gunmen.'

Craigie grinned wryly.

'If you're right, I'll sack you. Now—the terms of the job. There's not much in it, but that won't worry you. A thousand a year and expenses—expenses unlimited, of course.'

'My bank's the United,' said Kerr. 'Put what you like in there. I'm not hard up. Are there any orders?'

'Find Marlin, that's all.'

'Do I get any help if it's wanted?'

'I'll introduce you to one or two of the others,' said Craigie, 'not here—at the Carilon Club. Then you can have police assistance whenever you want. But try to do it through Superintendent Miller; usually he works with us. It wouldn't be a bad idea,' he added, rising and tapping out his meerschaum, 'to go and see Miller now. Give me five minutes.'

In that five minutes, Bob Kerr was able to look about him. He had a feeling he would be seeing a great deal of this room —the only office of Department Z—in the future. It was rather large, and simply furnished: one end as an office: the other—where a fire blazed cheerfully—very much like any bachelor's living room. There were two easy-chairs, a built-in cupboard and a small table strewn with all manner of objects from a honey-pot to an automatic revolver.

Later, Kerr was to learn that Craigie had a flat in Brooke Street, but used it rarely—his men in 'Z' said never—for his office hours were non-existent, and there was seldom much respite between jobs.

* * *

Superintendent Miller and Bob Kerr sized each other up and the liking was mutual. The meeting was a brief one, as Miller was due to attend a conference with Sir William Fellowes and his Assistant Commissioners.

'Any time you need help, let me know,' he told Kerr. 'Got anywhere, Craigie?'

'No further than Marlin.' Craigie frowned a little. 'I wish your men hadn't let him go.'

'They'll wish it too,' said Miller grimly. 'Still, you'll get on to him soon, if I'm not mistaken.'

From Scotland Yard the two men walked back to Craigie's office, where they parted company, Kerr to go to the Carilon Club, to which he was no stranger, and Craigie to get back to the office and try and catch up some of the threads of the mystery.

Sabotage on a grand scale—but why? Where would it end, and what was the motive? And equally important, who was behind it?

Craigie was prepared for the next development, for there were few things he did not know ahead of the press. But the next morning's headlines carried a surprise for Bob Kerr, and he realised in a flash that it must be connected with the rest of the trouble.

Geneva was winding up a session in which one of the many 'final' inquests on the Italo-Abyssinian War were held. Decriers of the League of Nations had splashed headlines ridiculing the inquest; supporters of it called as stridently for a definite repudiation of Italian claims to Abyssinia, and a declaration that the annexation to Italy was illegal. The League's final decision would, it was generally acknowledged, be indeterminate.

In the event, the decision was crowded out of the headlines by the sensational announcement that an *agent provocateur* had been busy touting for armament orders, that his name was Baertin, and that he represented certain American manufacturers. So much was not sensational; that these men existed, agents of most of the larger Powers, was generally acknowledged. The sensation came when three smaller countries announced that they had tried to place orders with Baertin some weeks before and had not been accepted: and that America was arming herself quickly and preparing for war.

The effect of this on the English people was not startling. Nor was the British Government unduly perturbed. In the first place, Baertin was probably lying. In the second, it was possible he represented another Power than America—and there were several Powers admittedly arming to the teeth, whose export orders might well be cancelled because home consumption was excessive.

Kerr was concerned by the announcement; Craigie was non-committal; but Mr. Gregory Marlin was inordinately pleased. It was what he liked to call the first step in the fruition of his plans.

For the first time in his life, Gregory Marlin was displeased with his appearance. He had always taken a peculiar pleasure in the fact that, while far from handsome of feature, he was at least arresting to look at. Now, he would have given worlds to be able to mix with a crowd and pass unnoticed. He did not fully realise that he was one of many who had suffered from the devastating effect of Department Z, that although the Department had been so much below strength it had already forced him to flee from his usual haunts and take cover. It was no pleasure to know that he had a reasonably safe hiding-place.

He did allow himself a smile of self-congratulation at the way he had escaped from his Hendon house. Once he had discovered the police were watching it, he had made up his mind to get out of their reach, and the fate of the Daimler's passengers had strengthened his determination. A brief tele-phone conversation with Benson had been enough: later, he had left his house with a letter in his hand, obviously making for the nearest pillar-box. The two plainclothes men had followed him—but incuriously; never dreaming he would not return. The big saloon Benson had promised had drawn up as he pushed the letter into the box. He had turned, waved to the policemen and climbed into the car, which was lost almost before the watchers realised they had been tricked. Half a mile away, he had transferred to another car...

Marlin's other house, known as 'Common View' was at the top of Putney Hill, near Wimbledon Common. He had bought it—under an assumed name—several years before, when he had dabbled in crime for the first time and been far-sighted enough to see the need for a hide-out. It was run by two middle-aged women and three men, all of whom were connected with Benson. He had been careful never to visit the house except in a closed car, and was reasonably certain none of his neighbours had ever seen him.

They had seen a Mr. Benjamin Piper, 'a retired gentleman,' who let it be known that he had rented the place from a Mr.

Peterson, who lived abroad. Piper had good reason to be thankful for the help of Marlin and Benson, and he was not likely to squeal: he had once committed a murder, of which Benson had ample proof.

Benson, as Marlin had once said unpleasantly, could be described as gang-leader. He had a dozen or more gunmen on his books, and hired them out as and when required. Until his association with Marlin, most of his activities had been carried out on the Continent. His men had been shipped abroad, done their work, and returned without fuss—and he preferred it that way. But the bribe dangled in front of his eyes by Marlin had been too enticing. A hundred thousand pounds was a lot of money; even for Benson, who was considerably wealthier than most of his associates would have supposed.

Until the failure of the attempts to kill the Arrans and Gordon Craigie, he and Marlin had worked together well enough. But since Marlin's loss of temper, there had been a distinct coolness between them. Miller's visit had made Marlin see how much he needed the other man, and when Benson called at the Putney house—about the time Craigie was introducing his new agent to Miller—he greeted him with disarming frankness.

'I was annoyed,' he said, by way of apology. 'My dear fellow, you mustn't take me seriously. But the morning papers show how well things are developing for us, we must work together even more closely.'

'You'd better not get annoyed like that again,' Benson said harshly, 'or you won't be working at all. There are limits to what I'll take from you Marlin, and don't forget it.' Abruptly changing the subject he sat down. 'The Geneva show's just what we want. Have you heard from Northway, yet?'

'No—not a sound.'

61

'And Craigie flew over,' grunted Benson. 'He's got something from Northway all right. Much danger there?'

'Northway didn't know enough to do any serious damage; only to make Craigie know I'm involved.'

'Will it still take you three weeks?' Benson asked.

'We might do it earlier,' Marlin said. 'But I think we ought to keep quiet for a bit, Benson. Craigie nearly caught that car last night.'

'That wasn't Craigie.' Benson had suspected from the first stop-press announcement that Kerr's flight passenger might be Craigie. He had been at Heston for the 'plane's arrival and had followed the Talbot to Piccadilly after telephoning instructions to his men to watch for it and 'look after' its occupants. And he had witnessed the fire in which three of his best men had been killed. His only concern was that the efficiency of his organisation was impaired. 'That was Kerr. I've met him, and if he's working with Craigie, that means Craigie's practically at full strength again.'

He scowled. 'I've run my outfit for seven years,' he said, 'and I've never learned a lot about Craigie. This is the first time I've ever come up against him, and I don't like it.'

'All the more reason we should lay low.'

'Blast you, Marlin,' Benson snarled. 'You trying to teach me my job? Get them—or they'll get us. A couple of days would be different, but too much can happen in three weeks. But *you're* all right, now.' The tinge of contempt in his words made Marlin flush. 'You look after the money and I'll do the rest.'

'You haven't done much, so far,' Marlin snapped.

'You can't win every time. One of the Arrans is in hospital, but anyhow they don't matter now. They just do as they're told: the men we've got to get are Craigie and Kerr.'

Some twenty minutes later, Marlin was talking on the telephone to a certain gentleman about money, and Jacob Benson quitted the Putney house. On the surface, at least, they were still good friends, and Benson was telling himself in his cold-blooded way that he couldn't expect a man who'd never done a killing to be happy about it. But if the money was to come, the blood must run. And Benson was avaricious.

6

A TRIP TO KENT

No one was more pleased than Bob Kerr that nothing happened on the surface for forty-eight hours.

Craigie was more anxious for developments: he had no desire for Gregory Marlin to disappear completely and the mystery consequently to remain unsolved. But he was pleased enough with the breathing space. For one thing, it would give his new man a chance of getting to know those agents who would be working with him.

For his part, Kerr wanted the rest. The Atlantic flight had been one of the worst long-distance hops he had ever tackled. On top of that, the shaking-up he had endured during and after the car chase had left his nerves raw and created a tendency to over-hasty decisions and action, and he was well aware of the fact.

Robert McMillan Kerr had flown nearly a hundred thousand miles had rubbed shoulders with death a dozen times without actually dying; had scars and mended bones as souvenirs of crashes, and a mind that worked at mercurial speed in moments when a second's delay might mean the difference between life and death. He was quiet to the point of taciturnity, completely indifferent to hero-worship and unaffected by success. He had a sense of humour, but it had its blind spot.

Kerr had always been too busy to worry much about home life or women. The latter he admired but preferred to keep at a distance, although he could be a captivating companion and, if he put his mind to it, a reasonably good conversationalist. He remembered neither mother nor father, but had two sisters, whom he visited twice a year and was something of a favourite with an assortment of nieces and nephews. He had friends, practically all of them members of the Flying Club or their set, although he had met many men in his travels. He was rich enough to afford to frequent the Éclat and the Carilon Club if he chose, but rarely did choose. Most of his flights had been solo and consequently he had come to depend on himself alone and never hankered after companionship. Essentially an individualist, his one lurking fear was that he might find himself fettered by discipline; but he had seen enough of the Chief of Department Z to know that fear was groundless. In effect, Craigie had told him to do what he liked, how he liked, but to expect no obituary, and he looked forward very much to meeting the other agents.

There had been a time when Gordon Craigie had not allowed his men to meet each other: when all of them had been known by numbers and frequently ate and drank with other agents, without knowing they were detailed on different branches of the same job. It had often happened, however, that Craigie had found it necessary to have half-a-dozen or more men at the same place and rubbing shoulders; consequently, a small coterie in London knew each other as Craigie's men.

There were dozens of smaller agents who still worked quite anonymously; on getting information. His picked men, including the Arran twins, Carruthers, Davidson and Dodo Trale, he used for serious action.

Kerr remained alert as he walked to the Carilon Club: for if there had been one machine-gun attempt, there might be more. It was the first time he had ever walked on *terra firma* feeling that any moment might bring danger, and he rather enjoyed the novelty. Nothing happened, however, and he entered the Club—that male stronghold where women were only admitted, grudgingly, on two afternoons a week— and as Craigie had instructed, asked for Timothy Arran.

He was taken to the billiards room, and he entered it conscious of the brief but none-the-less thorough scrutiny of four pairs of eyes, and a sense of being tried by his peers. As the attendant closed the door behind him, one of the four men came forward, hand outstretched.

'Hello, there! Kerr, isn't it?' Timothy shook his hand vigorously. 'I'm Arran. And you might as well meet these other louts. They don't matter much but they'll probably get in your way some time or other and you'll want to know who to shout at.'

Bob Kerr grinned. But he was well aware that these were men who had worked with the Department for years—and that he, a newcomer, had been virtually put in charge of them. Not one of them, he noted, hinted or looked as if the fact was even remotely resented.

The languid Davidson smiled his lazy smile. The spruce, fair-haired Carruthers sketched an amiable salute. And Dodo Trale, stockier than the others and not quite as tall, wondered if he could drink a beer?

'Try me,' Kerr invited, and they all grinned.

'Large or small, Kerr?' drawled Wally Davidson. 'Good!' There was a brief pause, while he dispensed the beer expertly into the tankards standing ready on a side-table. Kerr guessed that this was a kind of Department Z initiation, and his heart warmed to the four: they were, he felt, men after his own heart.

'Here's how,' said Timothy Arran as the tankards were raised. 'And may Mr. Marlin die a nasty death.'

Kerr took his beer like a man of long practice, but drew a cry of protest from Davidson when he refused a second pint. Arran informed Davidson that he was getting to be an officious bounder and would he kindly keep quiet? Carruthers supported Wally warmly and Dodo Trale claimed that he had the deciding vote—and offered to sell it to the highest bidder. All in all, Kerr was almost sorry when, twenty minutes later, the party broke up, and he found himself with Davidson and Arran in the former's Lagonda on the way to the latter's Auveley Street flat. They were safely there and Kerr had been introduced to Heggson as a man who was always welcome, before there was a suggestion of seriousness in Timothy's manner.

'Well, well,' he said when the door closed behind Heggson, 'other things apart, I'm damned glad to have you with us, Kerr. I heard'—there was a twinkle in Timothy's eye—'about the little do last night. Nothing like working fast. What do you make of things?'

'They look awkward,' Kerr suggested.

'Damned warm,' admitted Timothy. The trouble is, you know, the Department's becoming known. This Marlin customer must have learned a whale of a lot to have started in on us when he did.'

'Doesn't look as though he's going to stop at much.'

'He isn't,' Timothy said bleakly. 'My brother caught a packet, but I suppose you know that. Well...'

The three of them talked around the situation at considerable length, and Kerr returned to the Flying Club happily certain of the support he could have for the asking, and wondering just when and where the next move would come.

It came from Superintendent Miller, via Toby Arran, forty-eight hours later. Toby was making an unexpectedly speedy recovery, and when Miller called at the hospital he found Toby able to give a reasonably good description of the man who had shot him. Timothy entered the ward a few minutes later and was jubilant at the great improvement of his twin. He told him about Kerr, and passed the opinion that their new colleague was the goods, before leaving the hospital to report to Craigie.

Miller, meanwhile, circulated the description of the gunman. It was towards evening when a report came in that the man had been seen near Dover. The constable concerned had been about to flag the car down when it was driven at him, forcing him to jump for safety. He had taken the licence number, but although an order to stop a dark blue Morris 20 saloon, number 9 ZY 213, had been flashed throughout the country, it was not reported.

'So our man might be in the Dover neighbourhood?' said Kerr. 'And if he's changed the number of course, he might be anywhere. If he's looking for a chance of getting abroad he'll use some kind of a disguise, I suppose. The trouble with a man who's used to it—and he seems used to it—is that he'll be able to disguise himself well enough for general purposes, and he'll be prepared with passports.' Kerr pursed his lips after this comparatively long speech, and hunched his shoulders.

Craigie waited for him, and Arran silently proffered cigarettes. Kerr said: 'No thanks. Craigie, have you a map showing the situation of all naval and military bases? Aviation, munitions and so forth?'

'Yes,' said Craigie, answering both questions. As he rose and made his way to the files at the far end of his office, he added: 'You'd better come over here: we can spread it out on the desk.'

Moments later, the three men were pouring over it together. It was completely straightforward as far as the charting of rail tracks and roads went. But scattered all over it were heavy dots in a variety of colours, and Kerr and Arran were soon intently studying the key provided at the foot of the map.

Red: Naval ports.

White: Army encampments.

Blue: Air Force bases.

Green: Munitions factories, various.

Pink: Petrol stores over 5,000 gallons.

Mauve: Aeroplane factories (military).

Yellow: Heavy gun manufactories.

Grey: Gas manufactories (including protection).

Black: Shipbuilding yards.

Brown: National Defence bases.

Buff: Various subsidiary departments.

Government-owned: marked (1). Privately-owned: marked (2). Government-subsidised: marked (3).

'So there's a large petrol store near Dover?' Kerr mused. Adding, as Craigie nodded approval of his line of thought, 'How many men can I have?'

'Four,' Craigie told him, promptly. 'You know them all.'

'That's great,' Kerr thanked him. 'Can you get them together?'

'I'll arrange for them to meet you at the George Hotel, Dover, in three hours: you won't get there much before that.'

'If Arran's free right now,' smiled Kerr, 'We'll be there in under two.'

'Of course,' said Kerr to Arran, who was at the wheel of his Frazer Nash and doing justice to that prophecy, 'it isn't likely that our man's trying to flee the country right now. He wouldn't have gone to such trouble to make himself invisible here, unless he wanted to stay—or needed to. Which suggests that he still has unfinished business to carry out.'

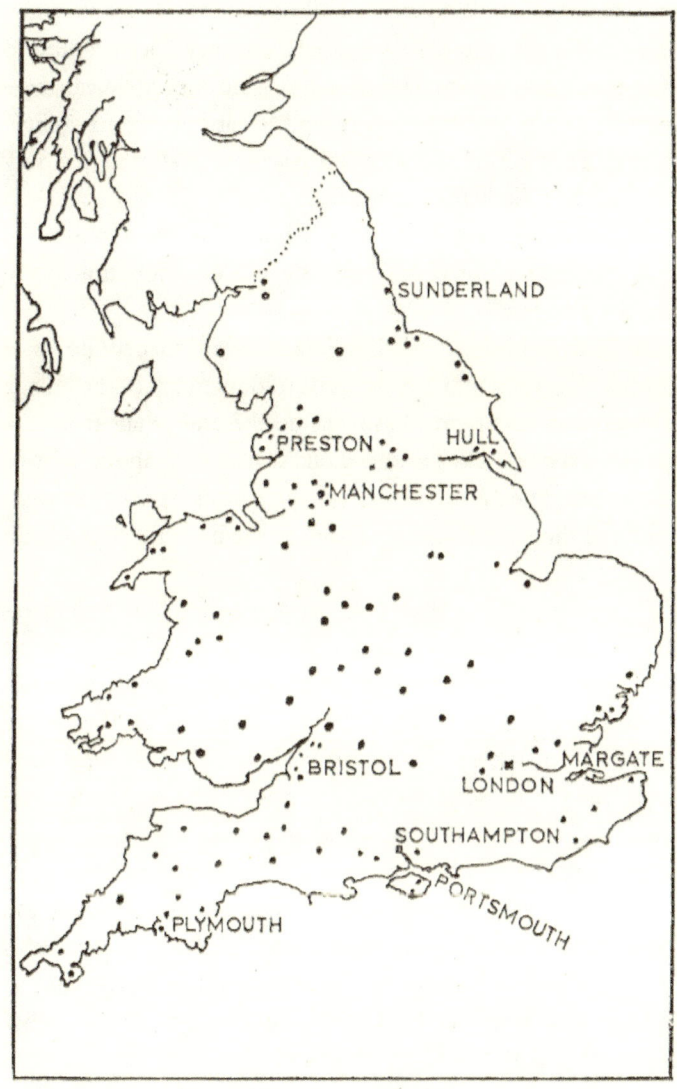

He was silent for several seconds, and Tim invited: 'Well, go on—don't stop there.'

Kerr chuckled. 'Yes, well—we know he won't scare easily: no one who uses guns the way that customer does is going to have much fear of the law. But he'll know pretty fast, if he doesn't already, that the Department is hard after him, so he'll be in more of a hurry now to finish what he's started. It's only then that he's likely to try a getaway.'

'So we've got to look out for fireworks?'

'I shouldn't be surprised,' said Kerr. 'Hey—slow down! We take the next left.'

A few seconds later the Frazer Nash turned down a second-class road which a signpost told them led to the village of Pockham. The petrol base was a mile and a half from the village, between Dover and Folkestone, and about a mile inland. Both men grew silent as they drew nearer. If they were right and their man was interested in the base, they could run into big trouble.

They reached the place without going in. It was a comparatively large encampment and probably a hundred men were inside the high, steel-mesh fence that marked its boundaries. Warning signs abounded. A few tin buildings in the centre showed them where the petrol was stored—in underground tanks, for the most part—and a series of smaller sheds close against the fence looked like living quarters.

'We'll fetch the others,' Kerr said, 'and then come back.'

Arran nodded as they finished a complete circle of the fence, and returned to the road. It took them fifteen minutes to reach Dover and locate the George Hotel, and eager not to be long away from the Pockham base, Kerr grunted his relief as Timothy said: 'There's Wally's bus!'

Parking the Frazer Nash beside it, they entered the lounge and spotted Davidson's tall figure at once.

Trale was there, too—and someone else Kerr didn't know. He was naturally surprised at Timothy Arran's sudden:

'The little devil!'
.For he had never met Miss Penelope Smith.

7

TROUBLE AT POCKHAM

Timothy was really taken aback. He found it
momentarily impossible to reconcile Penelope's
appearance here with the fact that she had boarded the Calais
boat at Dover.

'And what are *you* doing here?' he demanded, ungracious in
his astonishment.

'I followed you,' she told him, simply.

As Timothy gaped, Wally Davidson murmured drily:

'Penelope—meet a friend of ours, Bob Kerr. The famous
flyer. Kerr—Miss Penelope Smith.'

'How do you do?' said Penelope, her eyes widening as she
realised why the man was familiar. She had told herself the
moment she had set eyes on him that she had never seen him
before, and that he looked the most disagreeable man she had
ever met—for one, that is, who looked as though he could be
affable.

'How do you do?' Kerr echoed distantly.

He was certainly the most aloof man she had ever met,

Penelope thought, and if this was the result of fame she would rather meet people of whom the world knew nothing.

'But look here,' Timothy broke in at last: 'It's too bad. Pen! You ought to be in Cannes. What on earth brought you back? And what the deuce,' he added, suddenly realising it, 'do you mean by saying you followed me?'

Penelope smiled and sighed. This was proving more difficult than she had imagined, for although Davidson and Trale had been friendly enough, they had shown no real pleasure at her presence there and clearly considered her return a breach of faith, to say the least.

'I wanted to know how Toby was,' she said obstinately.

'Did you, indeed?' Timothy muttered, 'Did you indeed!' he repeated, more loudly. 'Came back from Cannes to enquire, eh?'

'I didn't go to Cannes. I felt I couldn't, so I wired Aunt I'd been delayed.' She smiled again, then ventured an almost penitent: 'Tim, I hope I haven't put my foot in it?'

'It wouldn't surprise me,' said Tim bitterly.

It was an offensive thing to say, particularly for Timothy Arran. What Penelope had no way of knowing was that the only other girl Timothy had cared for at all had been killed, and the memory was not a pleasant one. True, she had been more mixed up in Department Z activities than Penelope, but Tim was bleakly aware that Marlin and his friends were not likely to be respecters of persons or sexes.

Seeing Kerr smile, Penelope bit her lip and coloured.

'I think,' she informed Tim icily, 'I know when I am not wanted.'

She turned sharply away, pushing past Dodo Trale before he could move, and stalked out of the lounge.

'A bit hot, Tim, wasn't that?' drawled Davidson.

'Supposing it was!' snapped Arran, already regretting his

boorishness and furious with himself for it. 'Do we want to be saddled with a woman to look after?'

'Steady, you fellows,' Bob Kerr intervened, smiling, 'Sorry and all that—but we've a job on hand. I think we'll take both cars. You two will wait outside the camp—there's plenty of shelter from the woods there—and Tim and I will see what we can learn, inside. Craigie said the O.C. will be expecting us.' He was already moving towards the door. 'We don't want to lose any time.'

Timothy was the only one to give any further thought to Penelope. The others, keyed up at the promise of action, concerned themselves with thoughts of Pockham Camp alone.

Davidson and Trale took the Frazer Nash, since it would be easier to conceal, and the other pair drove ahead in the Lagonda. At the camp entrance they gave their names to the sentry, and were promptly passed through. Obviously Craigie's instructions had been received.

Colonel Martinson was a small, pompous man of middle-age, and already that day two very important officials—Sir Kenneth Halloway and Sir James Cathie—had pestered him on a tour of inspection. And his irritation at this further disruption of his daily routine was in no way lessened when Kerr cut short his fussy greetings with an abrupt:

'You know why we've come, sir?'

'Well, yes, of course—naturally! Enquiries from Whitehall. But if I may be frank, Mr. Kerr, I see no reason why Whitehall should suddenly be so interested in us down here. I'm sure we have never given the slightest cause for complaint...'

Kerr cut him short again:

'Have you had any trouble, lately?'

The colonel bristled.

'Just what do you mean by trouble?'

'Insubordination. Alarmist propaganda. Suspicion of sabotage—anything. The matter's important, Colonel.'

'I don't imagine you would be sent down here without good reason,' said the colonel, testily. 'But I can assure you that if there had been anything to report, you would have heard of it.'

'Nothing out of the way happen this morning?' Kerr persisted, curt to the point of rudeness.

'No. Good God, man, what *is* this? What *should* have happened?'

'You've had no strangers here, to-day, for instance?'

'None—none at all. Unless,' the colonel smiled bleakly, 'you find anything sinister in the visits of two senior Government officials, or a tobacco company's salesman.'

'What time did the salesman come?' Kerr asked sharply.

'The salesman? Why, eleven o'clock, as nearly as I can say.'

'A stocky man, was this? Fleshy, brick-red face, and a moustache?'

Timothy Arran had been watching the colonel's face during the exchange, and saw him gape now in obvious recognition.

'Good heavens!'

'Right?' said Kerr, and at the other's nod: 'Thank you, Colonel Martinson. And now I'll be glad if you can help me with some other information.'

Martinson could be concise, as he proved in the next three minutes. He seemed to realise suddenly that this was more than just one more sample of Whitehall red tape, and he showed that he had a keen sense of observation.

It seemed the salesman had made several attempts recently to interest the company canteen in a particular brand of cigarette, and the colonel had ordered his canteen sergeant to report next time the man bothered him. He had that morning made it clear that he would not stand for any pestering of his men to purchase specific brands of any goods, and he had not minced his words in the process. The man had first been seen about four days before, and was staying at the Crown Inn, Pockham.

'The devil he is!' Kerr grabbed the telephone and snapped as the switchboard answered: 'Dover Police!'

They were on the line at once, and he said quickly: 'Kerr, from Whitehall, speaking. You've had word, I think? Good. I'd like you, please, to send a dozen men at once to the Crown Hotel, Pockham. Plainclothes, if you can manage. I'll be there. How long do you think it would take?'

'About an hour,' said a businesslike Inspector, who clearly knew that Special Branch requests could rarely afford delay.

'Try to make it sooner,' Kerr urged. 'Goodbye!'

He was smiling as he replaced the receiver, his earlier tension quite gone.

'Sorry to be so abrupt, Colonel, but this matter is urgent. That man might be very dangerous. Will you be so good as to ask your men to keep a look-out—and, if they do sight him, put him under arrest until the police arrive?'

The message that had arrived only twenty minutes before these two men had read: 'Offer Kerr every possible assistance,' and was approved by initials that brooked no denial.

'Yes, indeed,' said Martinson. 'Be glad if we can help, Mr. Kerr.'

'Good man.' Kerr was moving towards the door as he spoke. 'Come on, Tim. I'll look in again, sir, or telephone you.'

Wally Davidson and Dodo Trale saw the Lagonda coming and drove to meet it. Kerr slowed down to bellow, 'The village!' and then trod hard on the accelerator.

Davidson grinned and said: 'He's the goods, all right!' then turned the Frazer Nash to follow.

Kerr slowed down again as he entered the High Street of Pockham; a fast-moving car, pulling up sharply outside the Crown Inn, would naturally alert anyone connected with the florid-faced man, who might be there.

The landlord of the old pub was slow of action and slower still of speech.

'Anyone staying here, sir?'

Kerr waited edgily as the innkeeper paused to think.

'Why, yes, sir,' he finally answered. 'Reckon you might say as there's several. There's Mr. Kirby, been here these ten years—'

'Someone who came recently?' Kerr prompted.

'Ah, that'd be Mr. Kelly, sir. Funny, having two names with a "K", I says to...'

'Is he still here?'

'Why, no, sir. He left about midday, I reckon.'

'Damn!' muttered Timothy Arran, breaking his silence.

'Why, sir, was it import...?' began the man. 'Well, I'll be danged!'

For Kerr had paused only to leave two half-crowns on the bar, and both he and Tim were out of the door in a flash.

'Well?' Tim queried, outside.

'I don't like the look of it.' Kerr climbed into the Lagonda and beckoned to Davidson. 'If this Kelly's gone, he's either finished his job or been scared off. I can't imagine Martinson scaring anyone off, so I repeat: it looks nasty. Davidson—hang around, will you? I'll phone a message to the George, or come back for you. Meantime, tackle our landlord and see what you can find about his Mr. Kelly.'

'Done,' said Wally. Adding, in a murmur that was lost in the hum of the Lagonda's engine as Kerr started back for the camp: 'I say it again—the goods!'

Kerr went as fast as possible, on the narrow roads.

'I'm worried, Tim,' he admitted. 'I wish I'd stayed a bit longer with the colonel. He'll be pleased to see me!'

It was not Kerr's fault that he had no opportunity of putting that prophecy to the test. He blamed himself, but no-one else did. It just happened.

They were in sight of the base when they saw the first huge plume of smoke. Kerr jammed on the brakes, a sixth sense telling him what to expect, and Timothy's face turned white. For in front of their eyes, one of the main storage tanks burst upwards and outwards. A tremendous cloud of black smoke billowed into the air, and through it, yellow tongues of flame were clearly visible. They saw one soldier a hundred yards from the tank blown off his feet and carried fifty yards away, where he dropped and lay still. Two tin buildings were whirled into the air and fell in sections, clattering and banging, while the rumbling explosion was repeated again and again as the other tanks went up.

The Lagonda was lifted off its wheels a yard into the air. Providence alone, both Kerr and Arran were fully aware, had saved them from disaster. Arran had gripped the sides to keep himself from being flung out, and still held on grimly. Kerr just sat, his hands on the steering-wheel, staring at the terror in front of him.

Hardly a building in sight was left standing, while jagged sections of walls and roofs were still clanging to the ground. The fence was smashed down in a dozen places, and dust and debris were still flying and falling everywhere.

The air was a black pall, now, broken only by those venomous flames which had taken hold more quickly and fiercely than seemed possible. Already, the wind was bringing gusts of heat-laden air towards them, and slowly, as if in a dream, Kerr pushed the gear-lever forward and the Lagonda moved.

He turned the wheel as sharply as he could and increased speed, circling the encampment and what remained of the steel-mesh fence. Arran didn't try to speak: he had no idea what Kerr was thinking, but was prepared to back him to the last. He himself was appalled by the ferocity of the explosion and the horror of the results.

The heat grew fiercer by the moment and now most of the smoke was high above the storage tanks. Beneath it, the flames were a solid mass of red, reaching out to spread throughout the camp. Timothy groaned as he saw the flicker of smaller fires dotted all about the ground ahead of them, and Kerr nodded tautly.

'God knows if we can do anything,' he said. 'But if you can yank that exting... Good man!'

Timothy glanced from the small extinguisher he already held, to the devouring mass of flames. 'But hang it...!' he began, and broke off, coughing, as the wind billowed the smoke about them.

'I'm not going to try to put it out,' said Kerr, with grim humour.

They were halfway round the camp before Tim Arran realised what was in his mind. Leeward of the flames, they might be able to get closer to the fire. The air here was clearer and they could see very much further.

Kerr jammed on the brakes.

'See what you can do,' he urged 'Bellow, if you want help!'

And now Timothy understood why the extinguisher was wanted. As he broke into a run, he saw Kerr take another and race towards the roaring flames.

There were about a dozen or more men sprawled about; some of them badly injured, most of them stunned. As the two of them drew nearer the main fire, the smaller blazes were more frequent. Kerr reached a man who lay unconscious with the flames singeing his hair: he used his extinguisher to good effect, moved the man as far as possible in a couple of heaves, and hurried on. Half a dozen times he repeated the move, and so did Timothy. What they saw shocked and sickened them, but at least they both knew they were saving some who must otherwise have perished.

In Robert Kerr's mind, at every moment, there was bitter reproach. If he had requested Martinson to make a thorough search of the tanks, and their approaches, this thing might have been avoided. In Timothy Arran's mind there was only wonderment that anyone could move as swiftly and effectively as this new man; any who lived would owe it to Robert Kerr.

Something more was torturing Kerr: a ghastly, haunting uncertainty—worse than anything he had ever experienced.

This thing had happened here, as they had feared it might. But how could he be sure it was not happening in a dozen other places, at this very moment?

8
NATIONAL CALAMITY

S teady on, old man,' said Wally Davidson, resting a hand on Bob Kerr's shoulder. 'You'll knock yourself up, and that won't help.'

'How many helping?'

'A couple of dozen, I'd say.'

'Keep going,' Kerr told him. 'We need more than that.'

It was half an hour after the explosion, and he had been working as he had never worked before. Davidson and Trale, who had rushed to the camp when they heard the explosion, had found him helping the injured with quiet fury and phenomenal stamina. His hair was singed, his face and hands burned, his coat and trousers torn and frayed. But he clearly meant to go on, and Davidson shrugged his shoulders and weighed in.

Another twenty minutes passed before Kerr stopped. By that time, assistance had arrived from Dover—brought by the first car-load of police coming to fulfil the Superintendent's promise of support. Several doctors were in attendance, and a dozen ambulances were already on the road to Dover Hospital, filled with men who had suffered dreadful burns or wounds. It was impossible to estimate how many men had been killed: three dozen or more had been pulled from the flames alive. A local journalist, one of the first men on the scene, had worked with the rest until more help had arrived, and then had tried to assess something of the damage.

Four farmhouses had been wrecked and a dozen occupants more or less badly injured, all within a mile radius of the base. Pockham itself had hardly a pane of glass left, and the innkeeper would return from the camp—where he had hurried to render what aid he could and taken with him two crates of whisky—to rue the broken bottles and the spilt beer and wines.

Over Pockham itself, there was a hush. Even the children stood in clusters, with pale faces and curious, wondering eyes; unable to understand the terror that had come. Throughout the village, there were women who sat dazed with shock or fighting against hysteria as they waited to learn if their men had suffered. And there were sweethearts as well as wives among those who hurried to the camp, dreading the worst yet desperately anxious to know the truth.

And all the time the pall of smoke over the countryside was like a cloud waiting to burst with thunder. For miles around, the oily black smuts covered the land and the trees and the hedges; it was as if that little corner of Kent was in mourning.

There was not much Kerr could do, once the authorities had taken charge. He had learned that Martinson was one of the victims, and was oddly relieved that he had been pleasant towards the man when he had last spoken to him. It was the only spark of cheer he felt for a long while after the explosion, and he could not have explained why it seemed so important.

He surprised the innkeeper by drinking a tumbler of whisky diluted with the merest spot of water, left Davidson and Trale to keep watching the place and, with Timothy, left for London in the Lagonda some two hours after he had arrived. He looked worse than he had after the crash in Grosvenor Place, but although he had allowed a doctor to dab his burned skin with some soothing lotion, he made no effort even to push a comb through his hair. Timothy had essayed a half-hearted toilet, but it was a woeful-looking pair who eventually reached his flat.

Kerr telephoned Craigie immediately.

'We're in too much of a mess to come over,' he explained. 'We'd be noticed by half Whitehall.'

'I'll be right with you,' said Craigie.

As they waited, Kerr roughed out a written report, adding to it the little Wally Davidson had learned from the innkeeper, Tippett, of the man they sought.

Ostensibly a salesman of cigarettes and cigars, Kelly had stayed at the Crown for ten days. He had visited other villages, as well as the camp, Tippett knew. He had always been pleasant—and free with his money.

There was one other small but significant point; Kelly had had a visitor on two occasions, and Tippett claimed he could be recognised as an American a mile off.

Craigie arrived, heard the story, and understood something of what was going on in the flyer's mind. Craigie had seen other men look like that when they had failed to stop a killing; either a single murder or a bigger outrage. But the work of the Department made it impossible for his men to be forever without a single slip, and he realised that while they were working so much in the dark it was impossible to prevent things like the Pockham disaster.

'Don't let it get you down, Kerr,' he told him quietly.

'I won't,' said Kerr, but there was horror in his eyes. 'I—if I'd thought to make a search...'

'You might have caught Kelly, and if you had it would have been justified,' Craigie agreed. 'No man can work miracles, Kerr. Do you think—' he paused a moment and his eyes held the airman's—'I enjoy sending my men out to that kind of job? Do you think I don't feel it, when a man goes out and isn't heard of again?'

'No,' said Kerr, and grimaced his apology. 'You're right.'

'Good,' Craigie nodded. 'Now, back to cases. There's one thing bothering me—'

'I know—why blow up a little dump like Pockham?'

'Exactly,' said Craigie.

'It would be easier to get at, than a bigger place,' suggested Timothy Arran slowly. 'They could get in, there, where they couldn't anywhere else?'

'Yes...' Kerr began. 'Of course, Martinson had this Kelly there this morning, and the man had plenty of opportunity to drop a time bomb anywhere. Particularly if he's been round the place often enough to know it. Men at the camp wouldn't be so careful with a familiar figure, either. But—and it looks as if Kelly is the man who shot Toby—he's not been staying at the Crown all the time.'

'It's not a long journey up to London,' Craigie pointed out. 'And he probably wanted to be near the camp until his job there was done. A man living temporarily in the village wouldn't arouse the same interest as one travelling to and fro. Well, I'll send the order out to keep eyes open for Kelly, but he'll have a pretty good idea there's a reasonably sound description going the rounds, and he'll be careful. Did he have the moustache, do you know?'

'Yes,' said Kerr.

'If he removes that, our chance of finding him is small,' said Craigie. 'I've men checking up every one of Marlin's clients, and we haven't found anything yet. The so-called American fellow might be anyone: it's no true indication. Well, now, anything else—?'

'There's one little thing,' Bob Kerr smiled, glancing at Timothy Arran. 'Miss Smith, Tim.'

Craigie already knew that Miss Penelope Smith had been close to extinction, and had been checked aboard the steamer for Calais. He said as much, and Timothy grimaced.

'Yes, I know. She's come back, drat her. I'm afraid I was a bit short, but I'd been telling myself she was miles away and safe enough. I mean—well, she's been seen and probably identified, and I don't like Messrs. Marlin and Kelly. Seeing her at Dover really got my goat. I think,' he ended gloomily, 'that I upset her.'

'The understatement of the week,' grinned Bob Kerr. 'I think she'd have enjoyed treading on you, Tim.'

'Thank *you*,' said Timothy coldly.

'Oh, that's all right.' Kerr was opening out, Craigie noticed, glad that the other had got on top of himself. It was essential for his men to harden themselves even against catastrophes like the Pockham affair: they could not afford to brood over failures. 'But—Tim: she claimed she'd followed you, right? Doesn't it strike you as odd she should have gone to London, watched you there and followed you down to Dover? Followed us, that is. She must have carried on to Dover when we turned off for Pockham, so—'Kerr was frowning, '—one, she didn't want to chance your seeing her on the Pockham road: and two: she knew you'd be going on with me to Dover.'

There was a moment's silence in the room, while Craigie rubbed his chin. Then Timothy broke the silence with a gusty:

'Are you suggesting *Penelope's* in this?'

'No...' said Kerr, although his denial did not sound genuine. 'But I should like you to find out just what brought her after you, Tim. Damn it, man, we can't let things like that go unexplained, can we?'

Timothy forced a smile.

'I can see you and me falling out before long,' he said, 'but I suppose you're right. That means, I take it, that I've got to hunt London for her. And when she sees me...'

'She'll be so sorry for you, the way you look right now,' said Kerr unkindly, 'that she'll forgive you.' He left the subject, although Craigie realised he was still very interested in Penelope Smith, and with good reason.

The same thing had jumped into both men's minds.

The Arrans had been Department men for a long time, and anyone who had ever known the Department or watched it working would have discovered that. Penelope Smith had come to London just at the time when Craigie's activities in America must have begun to worry Marlin and his friends—and thus just when the obviously unoccupied Arrans would be his likeliest choice to investigate any suspect situation at the London end.

True, that letter had come from Jeremy Potter—so far as they knew. But the timing of it had left the Arrans no chance to check with him whether he had actually sent it, even had they wished to.

According to the Arrans, Kerr was thinking, the girl had not been looking forward to her visit to the South of France. But then, if she wished to make a sudden reappearance seem more plausible, she could have given that impression deliberately. Dammit—they could not even be sure that the girl *was* Potter's niece: they had never seen her before.

Of course, he reflected, there had been that attempt to run her down when she had been with Tim. But then—and Kerr took a deep breath as the thought struck him—it had only *been* an attempt; and Tim had been the only one they fired at. Had the car missed them intentionally—an elaborately cunning ploy to ensure that no suspicion of any kind devolved on Penelope Smith?

Kerr left the flat with Craigie, and as they walked along together he voiced his suspicions aloud.

'It's a possibility,' Craigie agreed. 'Better go see Potter, yourself—if there's anything funny about this girl, he might be able to help you. Apart from that, he won't talk with just anybody: he's one of the old school.'

'What's his business?'

'Cotton and yarn. The Potter Mills were some of the biggest in the Preston district at one time, but they've not been doing so well, lately.'

'Cotton, eh?' mused Bob Kerr. 'Well, they use a lot of the stuff in armaments, not to say clothing. This girl's come from him. Just supposing, Craigie, that she isn't his niece. She might have been keeping an eye on Potter: might know the real niece and know about the letter through her—if it's genuine. It's even possible the real Penelope is at Cannes now.'

His next words, when they came, showed how thorough was his appreciation of the situation: 'Can you find out whether Potter's factories—or mills—have any Government contracts?'

'I think it certain they have,' said Craigie. 'I'll—but wait a minute. Halloway will know, and he's near here. We'll go and see him.'

'I seem to have heard the name?' queried Kerr.

'You'll have had a job to miss it, lately,' Craigie said drily. 'The Permanent Under-Secretary for Defence.'

Kerr had been away from home too much to know just how loud was the outcry for an adequate defence system for Great Britain. But Craigie's reminder was enough. Sir Kenneth Halloway had been very much in the news, of late.

He greeted them with an easy informality which somehow combined an undisguised respect and liking for Gordon Craigie with an equally obvious pleasure in meeting the famous airman.

Kerr had wondered if he might demur at giving information before a stranger—even one sponsored by Craigie himself. But the defence of Britain was clearly Sir Kenneth's favourite topic of conversation. He had, moreover, a remarkably good memory. He nodded immediate assent when Craigie asked whether the Potter Mills had any Government contracts.

'Yes, indeed. They're one of the major contractors—naval and military clothing. Not my meat officially, of course, but...' he grimaced wry admission of his preoccupation with the subject '—you can take my word for it.'

'That all you need to know, Kerr?'

'Ample,' said Bob Kerr, cheerfully.

'I didn't know you'd joined Craigie's Iron Men,' smiled Halloway. 'Be careful, Kerr.'

'He doesn't know how to be,' said Craigie. 'You might find him pestering you, Halloway—he's working on the sabotage business. You'll give him any help you can, without waiting for me?'

'Of course—any time,' said Halloway, warmly. 'The best of luck, Kerr. And if you can put your finger on Gregory Marlin, you might give him a little unofficial punishment.'

Kerr smiled.

'You know Marlin?'

'Who doesn't? And I'm particularly interested. The man had twenty thousands pounds' worth of bearer bonds from me the day he disappeared. He cashed them before going, of course.'

'Bad luck,' said Kerr. 'And you're not the only one to suffer, of course.'

'I'm certainly not. Cathie—' the Scottish Sir James Cathie was a man many people believed out of place in the Cabinet '—lost a bit, and I think Wishart suffered. Of course, he had a genius for making money—he probably made up in profits to his clients twice as much as he's filched. But he must have collected a cool hundred thousand pounds, before he went.'

They left Halloway at the Carilon Club—he was a bachelor —and walked to Whitehall. Kerr did not go into Department Z, and Craigie left him to prepare for his trip to the north. There was certainly a good chance that Jeremy Potter could give them some valuable information.

The journey from London to Preston would have taken most men five or six hours at least; it took Kerr an hour and a quarter, for he went by air in a specially commissioned Hawk. There were advantages in being known, in person or by reputation, at practically every airport in England...

The Hawk behaved perfectly and he reached the landing field at Preston—avoiding the big Liverpool airport to save time—at nine o'clock. He had arranged for a car to be waiting, and drove at once to Preston police headquarters, where he introduced himself. Craigie had already sent word through the Yard for him to be given every assistance, and he arranged for the Buick he had hired to be followed at a respectful distance by a police car with two armed men. He did not seriously expect trouble, but he was anxious to be prepared for it if it came.

It was dark, and he saw very little of Preston and its environs. Jeremy Potter lived in one of the residential suburbs on the Lancaster Road, and he reached the house soon after half-past nine.

The Larches was old but not gloomy and its porch was well-lit. From two or three of the windows lights shone cheerfully. He waited until he saw the police car pull up fifty yards past the house before he entered the short drive and drove slowly to the front door. The strains of a wireless programme, apparently from the basement regions, came to his ears. Everything about the place was so unexceptionably ordinary that his earlier conviction that he had struck something promising now seemed absurd.

'A wasted journey,' he told himself irritably, as the door was opened by a manservant.

'Good evening, sir.'

'Is Mr. Potter at home?' asked Kerr.

'I believe so, sir.'

'Ask him if he will see me, will you?'

Taking out a card, he scribbled on the back of it: 'On Government business'. That ought to make him more amenable to interruption, he told himself drily.

The man took the card with polite disinterest and ushered him into a small sitting-room off the entrance hall, then went silently out. Surveying the room, Kerr reflected that the house would be a positive treasure-trove for collectors: the furniture was both old and beautiful. The Potter Mills might be suffering a certain decline, but the family fortunes must still be fairly sizeable.

The door opened suddenly and he rose, prepared to see an old and probably crotchety gentleman. It was a shock to see instead a petite and attractive woman of perhaps thirty years of age, who greeted him with a pleasant enough smile. He could not immediately hide his surprise—could this be the *real* Penelope Smith?—but he recovered himself quickly as the smile widened.

'I'm sorry,' he explained, returning it, 'but I expected to see Mr. Potter. Is that possible?'

'I think so.' Her voice was attractive but just a little formal. She glanced at the card: 'Can I tell him what business?'

'I'm afraid it's confidential,' he said.

'I see,' She turned to go, then paused in the doorway to add with another quick smile: 'Mr. Potter likes me to see everyone who comes. He is a very busy man, and I'm afraid he is bothered a great deal by callers.'

She was probably only Potter's secretary, after all, Kerr decided wryly. Which would leave Miss Penelope Smith as much of an enigma as ever.

She had left the door open, and he waited as her footsteps echoed up the staircase and died away.

For a moment or two, there was silence—then suddenly, startlingly, the high-pitched cry of a woman. As he heard the agitated clatter of her feet on the stairs, he reached the door in one stride and stepped into the hall...

And told himself he had never seen such an expression of horror on the face of man or woman.

9

POTTER GIVES A CLUE

S he was half-way down the staircase when Kerr looked up; staring wildly ahead of her, her mouth agape: a travesty of the self-possessed young woman he had seen only minutes before. She was on the point of hysteria, he knew, and he took a dozen strides to reach the foot before she did. Gripping her arm, he shook it roughly.

'That's enough!' he snapped.

She stopped dead still and her eyes stared into his: the horror in them made him shiver.

'Steady,' he said more gently. 'Where is it?'

A dozen men would have asked what was the matter and thus risked an outburst probably impossible to stop. He had chosen the right approach. She drew a deep breath, and now he could feel her trembling.

'In—in his study.'

She was still shivering, her breath coming in deep gasps. But stiffly, automatically—and obviously unconscious of Kerr's helping arm—she started back up the stairs. They reached the landing and turned a corner. He could just see into a room through an open door, and the first thing that caught his eye was a telephone. So at least he could call for assistance if necessary.

She stopped a yard from the door.

'I can't,' she whispered. 'I can't!'

'All right,' Kerr soothed. 'You go downstairs and call the menservants.'

Kerr watched her stumble away—then drawing a deep breath, he stepped across the threshold. With one glance, he took in the signs of struggle: the overturned vase, the pipe obviously dropped while still alight—the carpet now smouldering around it and beginning to fill the room with acrid grey smoke. But the thing that mattered was stretched out by the fireplace: a ghastly sight, with the thickening scarlet circle vivid around its throat.

Kerr felt a strong desire to be sick. But he forced himself to cross the room—careful to touch nothing as he went—and throw open the window. He leaned out and the police-car driver, immediately alert, nodded sharply at his urgent gesture and pressed the self-starter.

Kerr withdrew his head and faced the room again. Potter, dead—murdered in his own hearth! One half of his mind was still hardly able to grasp the fact, but the other was already coldly weighing and assessing it. Potter was in this thing somewhere, he decided, grimly.

Footsteps clattered up the stairs and he reached the door as the first of the servants appeared. A stout man of middle-age, he was puffing hard and had obviously led the way as of right, and not because the younger men behind him could not have beaten him. His large, white face was set in alarm.

'What—what *is* it, sir? What has *happened?*'

'Steady.' Kerr pushed the man into the passage and pulled the door behind him. 'Is every manservant here?'

JOHN CREASEY

The large man regained his breath and his sense of his own position together.

'I insist, sir—!'

'Answer the question!' snapped Kerr. 'You are the butler, I presume?'

'Yes—yes, sir.'

'Good—then keep your wits about you. Are all the menservants here?'

The stout man glanced round at the other three and nodded.

'Yes, sir.'

'Right: one of you go down and open the front door—the police will be here in a moment.'

'The *police*?' The butler's eyes widened again. 'Sir, you really must tell me—'

'There's been a nasty accident,' Kerr explained, with a typically sudden switch to gentleness. 'It's best you don't go in there, Mr.—?'

'Oakwood, sir. But...'

'Because,' Kerr persisted, still gentle, 'there's positively nothing you can do. I'd suggest—ah, the police!'

Kerr had never in his life before taken any official part in a murder investigation. But the two detectives were obviously looking to him for a lead, and he gave instructions quickly and precisely.

'Telephone for the usual men,' he directed, 'and the local Inspector, if you can get him. If I were you, I'd keep these fellows up here. I'll go round with the butler and check that the women are all present.'

The taller of the two detectives nodded respectfully, and Kerr went downstairs with the trembling Oakwood. His first step was to ask for whisky and glasses. Oakwood clutched thankfully at his tot, and Kerr was feeling ready for his own. It was a grim business, and a lot had happened in a day.

The police reinforcements arrived in twenty minutes and included an Inspector by the name of Moor, whom Kerr liked on sight.

Oakwood had meantime rounded up all the female staff as well, but the Inspector's enquiries drew a frustrating blank.

None of the servants had admitted a stranger—or indeed, anyone at all—to the house that day. None of them had seen or heard anyone with Jeremy Potter. And as Kerr quickly discovered, there was no possible access to the study via the window.

Jeremy Potter was officially identified by Oakwood and by his secretary, Mrs. Lilian Trentham, who had worked for Potter for two years. A stiff brandy had steadied her considerably and apart from an understandable pallor, she seemed as self-possessed, an hour after the crime had been discovered, as she had been when he first saw her.

The Inspector from Preston had arrived by now, bringing with him a surgeon, a photographer and a finger-print man. Kerr watched all the formalities with considerable interest. The thoroughness of it all surprised and impressed him— although he did not disabuse the locals, who clearly assumed him to be an expert from the Yard.

He telephoned Craigie, who promised to try to get Miller to go to Preston in person, if at all possible.

'Meantime,' he advised, 'just do what you can. I've called Davidson and Trale back from Pockham—they can come up, if you like.'

'That's an idea,' said Kerr. 'But I don't think Arran had better come, do you?'

'No.' Craigie sounded grim. 'I'll keep him busy elsewhere.'

Kerr rang off with a feeling of real satisfaction. Craigie's confidence in his judgement and capabilities bolstered his own quite considerably—and intensified his desire to justify such faith in him.

The first thing, he told himself, was a talk with Mrs. Trentham. He asked Inspector Moor for a room in which he could interview her, and chose the small lounge where he had waited before the discovery of the tragedy.

The door closed behind the woman and she stared at him, still with a reflection, of that horror in her eyes. Kerr hated the job, but he dared take no risks and lose no time.

'Tell me,' he began, in that curiously gentle voice he could adopt. 'You've no idea of anyone with a grudge against Mr. Potter?'

'None at all. I can't understand it, I just can't.'

'So,' said Kerr. 'But there's an explanation somewhere and of course we've got to find it. You don't think the motive was robbery do you? I mean, Mr. Potter had not a great deal of extra money in the house to-day?'

'No—I'm positive he hadn't.' Mrs. Trentham smiled wanly, but Kerr noticed she tucked a wisp of hair into the thick braid about her head—a sign that she was beginning to think of her appearance again. 'He hasn't been well for the last few days and I've been to the bank for him. I usually go, so that's not very different, in any case.'

'He's not been laid up, has he?'

'Oh, no. Just out of sorts. After all he was sixty-five and more, and he's always worked hard.'

Kerr nodded. 'Was he off-colour before Miss Smith left here?'

He hardly knew whether to be pleased or sorry when she answered:

'No. He was well enough, then.'

She looked curious, and Kerr could understand it.

'I happen to know Mr. Arran,' he explained. 'I believe Mr. Potter wrote to him about Miss Smith?'

'That's right,' said Mrs. Trentham. 'I typed the letter.'

'I see.' Kerr smiled grimly to himself; that would cheer Timothy Arran, even if it burst the bubble of a plausible enough theory. 'Now—Mr. Potter hasn't seemed worried, lately?'

'Certainly not. I've noticed nothing different at all. Except...'

She broke off suddenly, and Kerr said quietly:

'It doesn't matter if the thing seems irrelevant, Mrs. Trentham. We'll have to go over a lot of useless details before we learn the truth.'

'Of course.' She flashed a smile that was wholly artificial. 'I was going to say he quarrelled with an old friend about ten days ago, but it was purely a personal matter...'

'Not on business?'

'Not as far as I know. It was with a Mr. Mayhew, an old friend, as I said.'

'And Mr. Mayhew's address is?' asked Kerr.

'He's—he's now living at a Manchester hotel, I think. He was a fortnight ago, anyhow, because I posted a letter addressed to him. Mr. Potter wrote most of his private letters himself.'

'I see,' said Kerr. 'You didn't notice the name of the hotel?'

'I'm afraid I didn't. In any case, I think May—Mr. Mayhew's gone abroad. I did hear some mention of it. He's interested in cotton production—he was going to Egypt, if I remember rightly.'

'I see,' Kerr repeated, and frowned. This Mayhew lived in an unknown hotel and was believed to be on the way to Egypt —or anywhere that cotton was grown. It was hardly helpful, and he went on more brusquely:

'Now, do you know of any other callers lately?'

'Well—Mr. Potter had a great many, particularly those days when he didn't go to the office.'

'Any strangers?'

'None to my knowledge. Of course, he occasionally opened the door himself.'

'Why?'

Kerr's abruptness seemed to disconcert her.

'I—I don't know. There were some callers, he preferred to admit to the house. I can't give you their names, I'm afraid.'

'Can't—or won't?' wondered Kerr. Aloud, he asked:

'Did they come by appointment, do you know?'

'They must have done. I was always asked to keep to my room for an hour when—when anyone was coming. I heard men talking to Mr. Potter, and I heard him let them in and show them out. But he was particularly anxious no-one else should be present, and I had to do just what he wanted, of course.'

'Of course,' Kerr echoed politely. This was discovery, with a vengeance.

'You've no idea what business they came on?'

'No—not the slightest idea.'

'I see.' Bob Kerr rubbed his chin thoughtfully.

'Well, Mrs. Trentham, I'd like you to let me have a list of all the people who have called, to your knowledge—and please, the names and addresses of anyone he's corresponded with. You can get that?'

'Most of it,' she nodded. 'Although as I've said, he did write some letters himself, without keeping copies.'

'Do the best you can,' Kerr urged, and opened the door. 'Thank you, Mrs. Trentham.'

The next hour passed slowly. With Inspector Moor, he questioned all the servants, and the story of the mystery callers was repeated over again. From time to time, the servants would all be required to remain in their own quarters for specified periods, while the master's visitors came and went. It was distinctly odd, and Kerr told himself it meant one of two things. Either Potter had been blackmailed, or he was working on some project in which he was particularly anxious his colleagues should not be recognised.

Kerr and Moor did their best to get some sort of timetable of the various calls, but it was useless. Sometimes it would happen once a week; sometimes daily. Three weeks before, the calls had been more frequent than usual, but no reliable dates were forthcoming. Oakwood, the butler, confirmed the quarrel between his late employer and the man Mayhew, but knew no more about the man than Mrs. Trentham. He was a cotton broker of some kind, Oakwood believed, who travelled a great deal.

'He's travelled a great deal too far for my liking, this time,' Kerr told Moor. 'Well, I'll leave it to you. A Superintendent Miller will be along before too long, and one or two others. I wonder if I could find something to eat?'

Moor said that he too would be grateful for a sandwich, and Oakwood provided an excellent impromptu snack. But as he ate, Kerr had an uncomfortable feeling that he should be somewhere else. Searching for the man Mayhew, for instance, he suddenly realised.

'Dammit!' he choked, from the midst of a sandwich. 'Sorry, Moor. But—do you know the Manchester police?'

'Yes—very well.' Moor, a burly Northcountryman, looked a query.

'Can you get them to find out what hotel a man named Mayhew was staying at, ten days ago?'

'There'd be more than one Mayhew.' Moor smiled stolidly. 'But they'll get them all for you.' He went at once to the telephone in the study—the only instrument in the house, Kerr had learned. The airman smiled at the speed with which Moor worked: in a different way, he was as effective as Davidson and the others in London.

Davidson and Trale, in point of fact, were dropping from leaden skies to the Preston airfield about the time the Manchester Police started their enquiries for the man named Mayhew. They reached the Larches at about half-past twelve, and one of the first things Davidson said was:

'If you don't get some sleep, Kerr, you'll fade out before this job's finished. Have some sense, man!'

'Thanks.' Kerr grinned tiredly. He could not deny the wisdom of that, and had no real desire to. So that at last, on the premises, the police looking after all straightforward work and the search for Mr. Mayhew proceeding satisfactorily, Robert McMillan Kerr sat in an easy chair and lit a cigarette.

Dodo Trale took it from his fingers two minutes later: Kerr was already fast asleep, and didn't stir even when Trale tucked a blanket around him.

If there was activity in Manchester and Preston that night, London was as busy in a different way. The affair at Pockham had been in the later evening papers and was already causing a stir among the public. That stir was nothing to the alarm it caused among certain members of the Cabinet, who met at 10 Downing Street soon after nine o'clock, and were still talking at one.

Some of them were irritated because Sir William Fellowes, who was present, claimed that nothing could be done and no useful decision reached without Gordon Craigie. But he was supported by the Prime Minister, Mr. David Wishart, and by Halloway, so none of the irritation was loudly expressed. No one present seriously thought the calamity was accidental.

Craigie's arrival, just after one o'clock, put new life into the meeting. Some of the Ministers had been in office for years but had never seen Craigie before; he was something of a legend in the House as well as Whitehall. His gaunt, rather hatchet face, his drooping lips and his serious grey eyes seemed in keeping with his reputation.

He nodded all round and sat down opposite Wishart; a thin, ascetic-looking man with sparse, silvery hair, who many people said would have decorated a chair at Oxford admirably but should never have reached Chequers or 10 Downing Street. Craigie knew better.

'Well, Craigie,' Wishart began, pushing cigars across the table: 'this is a terrible business. You told me you would like to see us.'

'Yes—thank you sir.' Craigie took a cigar and cut it slowly. 'Of course, this is part of the general sabotage; I needn't tell you that?'

'I suppose there's no doubt?'

'One thing is absolutely certain,' Craigie said incisively. 'The others might conceivably have been accidents. This one was deliberate.'

'Does that mean,' demanded Sir James Cathie, the Scottish Nationalist member, 'that you have actually traced something, Craigie? You've found the person who committed this dastardly outrage?'

'I can tell you what he looks like, but not his name. He was

JOHN CREASEY

traced to Pockham but escaped an hour or two before the explosion.'

'He shouldn't have escaped.'

'We're not dealing with shoulds or should nots,' retorted Craigie. 'The man did escape. It was very nearly a miracle that we traced him at all.'

'I think,' said Cathie acidly, 'we should have an explanation. Gentlemen?'

'I really don't think,' Wishart soothed—he disliked disruption in Cabinet ranks, and knew the Scotsman could be a Tartar—this is just the moment for that, Jamie. We're more worried about what's going to happen than what's already happened.'

Cathie subsided, but began to fidget again as Craigie sat smiling quietly to himself before saying:

'Yes, indeed—we're wondering what's going to happen. Well, I don't need to list the different crimes already committed but I will tell you that, including to-day's disaster, some two hundred men have lost their lives—in this country alone. The *Akren* disaster, closely allied to it—"

'Proof, proof!' Cathie muttered.

'I think we can take it for granted that the *Akren* disaster was part of a general campaign of sabotage,' said Craigie. 'But if you prefer not to, Sir James, that's entirely up to you. Some two hundred lives lost in England alone, serve to show you the ruthlessness of the organisation involved.'

'Well, of course, man!' said Cathie testily.

'And,' proceeded Craigie, aware that the rest of the meeting —seven Cabinet Ministers including the Home Secretary and the secretaries for War and Foreign Affairs, as well as Halloway, and Fellowes, the Chief Commissioner—were in sympathy with him, 'makes it clear that further disasters *might* come at any time. There's a direct motive, but we haven't found it.'

'My dear Craigie,' said the Scottish Minister, 'Russia—'

'Russia, Italy, Germany, Japan—all four possibilities!' snapped Craigie. 'We haven't had a direct line on any of them. The only thing we know is that a certain Gregory Marlin...'

'*Who?*' demanded Cathie, startled out of his pomposity.

Craigie smiled: he had learned that Sir James Cathie was one of Marlin's most influential clients.

'Gregory Marlin, Sir James. You know him, of course. He is connected with the organisation, and he has disappeared. We believe another man named Kelly is also connected, but we are not sure that is his real name. Marlin is our one definite hope. Every effort to trace him is being made, and his photograph will be in to-morrow's papers, together with the only available description of Kelly. For the rest—I don't need to tell you the position is serious. The Pockham catastrophe gives you an idea of what might happen. I am not exaggerating when I say that similar disasters—and very probably on a larger scale— are likely to come at any time. With one object in view, gentlemen: the inflaming of public opinion. Supposing, for instance, three other explosions should occur to-morrow. How would you keep the country quiet?'

Wishart eased his collar, and the faces of the others were grave. There was something ominous in Craigie's quiet, measured words:

'Frankly, gentlemen, I have an idea that before long we shall have more trouble—and soon after that, with the people incensed, we shall be told who is behind it.'

'*Told?*' echoed Wishart, incredulously.

'What I suspect,' said Craigie quietly, 'is that evidence will be put before the Government that a certain country has been responsible for the outrages, and public opinion will be so inflamed that there will be a general demand for war. I also think—' Craigie looked around the assembled company grimly, 'there would be a majority in the House in favour of it. Don't you, Mr. Wishart?'

'It would be a grave decision to take,' Wishart countered. 'But—if the incitement were great enough—'

'That's just it.' Craigie's voice sounded louder because of the hush. 'There will soon be agitation for war, gentlemen; I am as sure of it as I sit here. Now, you know the trouble has been world-wide. You know which countries have suffered most.'

'Don't beat about the bush, man,' snapped Cathie.

'I want you to see it for yourselves,' Craigie retorted coolly. 'Gentlemen—*can't* you see?'

The silence in the room was almost unbearable. It was broken at last by Wishart. The Prime Minister's face was very pale, and his eyes were fixed on Craigie's, as he spoke.

'You mean—*America!*'

'I mean America,' said Gordon Craigie.

10

DOWNING STREET FINDS
TROUBLE

Only Craigie, Fellowes, Wishart and Halloway were silent in the outburst that followed the Chief of Z's assertion, and Craigie's lips drooped familiarly as he listened. He had known that most of them would say that even talk of war between Great Britain and America was absurd.

He could have named almost any other country in the world and been heard with respect. But he had made a suggestion that warred with every preconceived idea in the minds of these men, and he knew they would not heed him. Unless...

Unless he could marshal words enough to show them how and why. Unless he could frighten them and pierce their smug complacency. Unless he could show *evidence*. And that was what worried him. He had none.

Wishart raised his hand for silence and as the indignant babble died down, nodded to him to continue.

'It seems absurd, gentlemen?' Craigie suggested. 'Well, perhaps it is. So was the start of the "Fourteen-Eighteen" war —but I am in more recent history. I want you, please, to think back to the last American Presidential Election.'

He could see he had their attention, and he went on quickly: 'You will remember the fierceness of that campaign, the fact that the country was at near fever-pitch throughout, that riots were quelled with difficulty in every state—and above all, that the issue was fought on foreign policy. As you know, the President was elected on a policy of isolation, after one of the closest votes ever known—although fully forty per cent of the American public voted against it. I could quote you a hundred instances where the late President Hafford was howled down for his insistence that America should not mix herself in European affairs. There were two strong voices in that, gentlemen: that of the Jews, and that of the Socialists—both groups incensed by the oppression prevalent in mid-Europe. Correct?'

There were murmurs of assent all round—even grudgingly, from Sir James Cathie. Craigie drew a deep breath: 'The election is over,' he continued quietly. 'And we have pretended that the issue is safe for the next four years. I doubt it. But that is only one aspect of the situation. Few men, if I may be permitted to say so, gentlemen—' Craigie's dry smile excused the unarguable claim—'have studied American politics more closely than I have: my agents over there, after all, report in detail on minor items that would not ordinarily come to light. They confirm what you and I can see, if we care to look, on the surface of America today: a tendency towards fanaticism as typified by those leaders who use mass hysteria to work their listeners to a pitch of almost religious fervour. On a dozen issues, that fervour has been evoked—most importantly, over foreign policy and national prosperity.'

He grimaced. 'You can see the dangers if a man of the late Huey Long's type succeeds in getting a wider power than Long ever had, and goes to the country on such issues as, one: Britain has committed an act of war—as with the *Akren* disaster, say. Two: America's isolation from European politics. And three: Fascism versus Jewry...'

But at this point, Wishart interrupted him. 'Surely,' he protested, 'those three issues are contradictory? I mean that if America wanted to interfere with European politics on the side of Jewry or anti-Fascism, she would naturally be with us —with Great Britain?'

'That's assuming, Prime Minister,' Craigie said, 'that there was reason behind the cry for interference—which means war. I'm putting it to you, gentlemen, that the only possible circumstances in which either Britain or America would declare war against each other would be a state of frenzied nationalism in which all grievances would merge together. There *is* no reason in a demand for war, but the unsettled state of American politics and mass-feeling would be the danger.'

'Yes...' Wishart agreed reluctantly. 'I'm prepared to admit there might be something in that. But Britain—my dear Craigie, there isn't much likelihood of an outbreak of fanaticism here! We haven't the same mixed population. We're not an easily-swayed people.'

'With respect, Prime Minister—you might have said the same thing in 1914,' Craigie pointed out. 'Although even then there was a general agitation against Germany; a deeper one than most of our politicians realised. Today, there is an equally strong agitation simmering—at the moment, directed against three things. First, the actions of the mid-European Fascist countries in the African war and the Spanish rebellion. Second, the repression of the Jews by the same regimes. And third, the reported activities of the Soviet Government. All three factors are being carefully nursed by sections of the press, and many of the editorials and front-page headlines are inflammatory to a point I consider both criminal and insane. Add to that the outcry when the Baertin business was published, and you can see that the public is being spoon-fed on American propaganda.'

'Yes.' Graeme, the Secretary for Foreign Affairs, spoke for the first time. He was a man of acknowledged ability and far-sightedness. That's true enough, Craigie. The thing's been building up for a long time. We're in for real trouble, if world affairs don't quieten down.'

'Exactly.' Gordon Craigie gazed around the table—and when he spoke again, there was in impassioned note in his words. 'Gentlemen: Great Britain is waiting for an excuse to show force—or her people are, even if her Government blinds itself to the fact. Give us one concrete example of hostile action from any country, and the chances of avoiding war are negligible.'

There was a brief silence after he had finished, and again, it was Wishart who broke it.

'I don't believe,' he objected, 'that responsible statesmen in this country or in America would commit such an indescribable folly as a declaration of war.'

'I am not thinking of responsible statesmen, sir,' said Craigie. 'I am thinking of men in public office bowing to the storm of public opinion. You can believe it or not, gentlemen, but the danger is acute; I will even say imminent. Supposing, Yelding,' he eyed the Secretary for War: 'we had the *Brittanica* —our *Akren*—blown to pieces with a full complement of officers and men? Supposing these things happened, gentlemen— which of you could stem the tide? And already a dozen smaller things have started; the fire is smouldering and waiting for the spark. Twenty men were deliberately killed—murdered—at Pockham. Are you going to suggest this was simply some form of industrial espionage? Or had it some deeper motive? Ask yourselves, gentlemen—ask yourselves!'

For several seconds, Craigie's voice echoed in the stillness.

Fellowes apart, he knew, there was hardly a man there who could say what he really thought.

'There is undoubtedly,' Wishart said, at last, 'something profoundly disturbing in this latest catastrophe, Craigie. But when you ask me to believe it is the beginning of an attempt to incite war between the two English-speaking countries, it is more than I can accept.'

'Why *should* they fight?' demanded Cathie.

'Any other power,' said Halloway, 'and I could understand it. The situation's dangerous, I know—and God knows I've never stopped trying to strengthen our National Defences. But—!'

He shrugged, and Craigie nodded. 'I know: it's absurd. I hope you are right gentlemen. But you are all convinced of danger of some kind. You asked me, some six months ago, to investigate the various occurrences of sabotage, and I have given you a considered opinion. You will no doubt expect me to continue to make every effort to find who is behind the campaign. So I want your help in at least one respect. I want all naval, air and military bases and ports to be protected as they would be in time of war—and I cannot be responsible, gentlemen, for the results if that protection is not afforded.'

The Rt. Hon. David Wishart and the Home Secretary, Sir Tristram Davies, watched the other members of the meeting prepare to leave. Both men were deeply worried: in their hearts they both realised that Craigie, of all people, would never speak as he had done without good cause. No-one, not even Craigie, had much to say: they spoke their good-nights glumly. Craigie and Fellowes were talking quietly together near the door, and would have been the first to go if Wishart hadn't called:

'Craigie—give me five minutes, will you?'

Craigie drew away as the footman opened the door, and

Sir Charles Garney and Arthur Simmersley—two Ministers without portfolio—were the first to step into Downing Street. A gust of wind blew rain into their faces and Garney muttered 'Brrr!'

It was the last word he spoke. The car that moved forward—driven, the watching police thought, by Halloway's chauffeur—suddenly roared into top gear as the driver tossed something into the porch. There was a single, blinding flash; an explosion that sent the windows smashing inwards, a splash of something wet across Yelding's face—Yelding himself was protected by Garney's body—and a blast of air that sent every man there staggering back. Then a sudden bellowing across the silence outside, the shrill piercing of police whistles, the backing of the high-powered engine and the screech of tyres as the limousine swung into Whitehall.

One of the most peculiar things about the Downing Street outrage was that Halloway's chauffeur, Johnson, was later found—doped but otherwise unharmed—among the bushes in St. James's Park. When he recovered consciousness, he told Craigie and the others that he had had Sir Kenneth's permission to leave the car outside the house for an hour, while he slipped away to meet his fiancée. He had been overpowered by a man who had sprayed the stuff—ether-gas—into his face, and remembered nothing else. Halloway confirmed giving the permission, but his feelings were not helped when Cathie said audibly that the Under-Secretary was a damned sight too easy-going: that if he hadn't been, this would never have happened.

'You're lucky they didn't use your car,' Craigie retorted sharply. 'Your man went off without permission!'

It was the truth; the sergeant of police on duty had reported it. Cathie was reduced to silence, but Sir Kenneth Halloway went home still plainly appalled for all that by the ghastly catastrophe.

Kerr awakened at six o'clock the next morning, somewhat stiff but considerably refreshed. He looked round in surprise for a moment, realised where he was and that he had fallen asleep while protesting he was not tired, stood up, yawned, and went to the door. It was open and he heard Wally Davidson say:

'Yes, I'll get him.'

'Craigie,' Davidson told him, turning as he entered, and Kerr's smile of greeting disappeared as he took the instrument. He needed no telling that something abnormal had happened, for Davidson looked like a ghost, and he spoke quickly into the mouthpiece.

'I can do with you, down here,' Craigie said, his voice sharper than Kerr had yet known it. 'You'd better fly. Bring Davidson with you. Leave Trale there. You've found nothing, I take it?'

'Nothing that won't keep a couple of hours,' said Kerr.

He did not wait to ask what was the trouble, but rang off and spoke to Moor, who had just entered the study.

'Can you find me a car, right away?'

'Aye,' said Moor, 'it'll be waiting.'

Kerr smiled his thanks and turned to Davidson—and his mouth set tightly as he heard Craigie's news of the Downing Street outrage.

'I see,' he said. 'Moving fast. Are you ready?'

Davidson nodded. They told Trale he was to stay, and left

the Larches within five minutes of the telephone call. Both of them were silent until they were racing down the empty road.

'Did you get a nap?' Kerr asked, then.

'Yes, thanks; a couple of hours.'

'Good. Thank heaven for it,' said Kerr, and a moment later, his lips curved in ironic amusement. 'When you've been busy before, has it been as warm as this?'

'Nearly,' said Davidson.

They did not speak again until they reached the airfield. Moor had thoughtfully telephoned to prepare the officials, who handed sandwiches and flasks of tea into the cockpit after the two men climbed in. Kerr said:

'I can do with that, thanks. Pull those chocks away, will you?'

The mechanic nodded and obeyed, and a minute later the little plane was moving along the ground. The storm that had raged in the south on the previous night had not reached the north, and the short flight passed without anything untoward, unless it was Kerr's handling of the Hawk. Davidson called it suicidal, although as they neared London he realised that Kerr flew almost by instinct; his apparent carelessness was really inborn confidence.

They passed over the green and brown countryside: England in the early Spring, and although neither man would have admitted it they were both thinking of the same thing. Someone—something—was trying to create chaos on these fair fields: disasters like the Pockham affair might come at any moment. Craigie and his men were fighting now more grimly, perhaps, than they would if the storm burst and they found themselves at war. As they flew, it struck Kerr that they might actually be passing over Marlin, or the man named Kelly, and they realised afresh the desperate need of finding one or the other of those men.

They spoke very little; Davidson's natural discursiveness had been arrested after the news of the Downing Street bomb-throwing, and Kerr was busy with his thoughts. He saw a dozen roads open for investigation, and smiled drily to himself as he realised that he could only follow one of them at once. That was good enough if he followed the right road, but if he mistakenly chose a cul-de-sac, he would be wasting valuable time. He was beginning to see how Craigie worked, and why he needed so many men.

They reached Whitehall *via* Heston Aerodrome two and a half hours after leaving Preston. Together, they walked past Great Scotland Yard towards that small, unimportant-looking door on the right. They saw a dozen men and women passing along the street and each of them wondered if yet another attack was coming. They were probably being watched, for Marlin would stop at little to get rid of Craigie's agents: Kerr had a brittle feeling that any minute might be his last.

They gave the necessary signal, on the bell, and the door opened. Both of them breathed more freely as it closed behind them. Davidson smiled and produced cigarettes as they mounted the stairs towards Craigie's room.

'We're doing well,' said Kerr, 'Thanks. This is an infernal trick of Craigie's, keeping us waiting here.'

'That man doesn't go wrong often,' said Davidson.

They had reached a landing from which a single door led; it was shut tight and they knew it would not open until Craigie had pressed a switch in his office. Craigie took no chances of being attacked in his room. The chances of any unauthorised person getting in were small, but not impossible; moreover, Craigie was prepared for trouble from all directions, both in and outside Whitehall.

The two agents waited for perhaps three minutes before he

opened the door. He stood on the threshold, his meerschaum in his hand, an expression that defied description in his eyes.

'Sorry,' he said. 'I was on the telephone. Come in.'

Kerr passed him, appalled by the greyness of his face, and his obvious weariness. Davidson whistled to himself; he had seen Craigie worried, but never anything like this.

'What's the trouble?' Kerr asked, as they sat down, Craigie in his own chair by the fire. When he was worried, he invariably hugged the warmth.

Craigie shrugged.

'Nothing; everything. We're close to a panic, and I don't like it. Have you seen the papers, this morning?'

'Haven't had time.'

'There they are,' Craigie said simply, motioning to his desk.

Davidson and Kerr rose together and walked to the desk. A dozen papers were there: all the national dailies and the more important provincials. Kerr read the headlines and could understand something of the burden under which Craigie was suffering.

Only one paper—the comparatively unimportant *Weekly Workman*—did not carry headlines that were a virtual demand for war. Even the Left Wing—and usually pacifist—papers stated in their leaders or front pages that the situation was ominous; that once the perpetrators of the outrage at Pockham and the murder of Sir Charles Garney and Arthur Simmersly were discovered, the act of reprisal must be severe.

The *Clarion*, usually one of the more excitable papers, had a leader that was more considered than most of the others, but which summed up the general opinion of both the left and right wing press. Craigie, watching the two men, smiled a little as he saw Kerr pick up the *Clarion*: Kerr had a habit of getting at the right thing without wasting time, Kerr took in every word rapidly. The leader ran:

'The two outrages reported on the front page, of equal importance from a political and international viewpoint and both equally tragic, both demand the most rigorous steps the Government can take. The Clarion voices the opinions of the people when it says that we have no desire for war. But if these outrages were instigated by foreign influence, then the countries or country responsible must be taught a sharp lesson. The declaration of war is a grave step, a terrible step when one pauses to consider the dangers and perils of gas and modern armaments, but if Great Britain is to retain the respect of the world there must be no hesitation now. A quick step and a decisive one is imperative.

'The responsibility of the Government is greater now than it has been for years. There can be no two sides to the question. England is virtually living in a state of war. There is no guarantee that further outrages on an even more terrible scale than that at Pockham will not be perpetrated. The Clarion, with all the knowledge of the gravity of the responsibility on the shoulders of the country's leaders, solemnly charges them, in the name of the people, to discover without delay who is responsible, and to act in no uncertain manner when they know. No one who does not deliberately blind himself can deny that foreign influence is at work; it is not for the press, but for the Government, to identify that influence and destroy it.'

Kerr put the paper down and walked slowly back across the office. Davidson followed him and Craigie surveyed them, both without speaking.

'Well,' said Kerr. 'What will happen?'

'What can happen?' asked Craigie wearily. 'War, Kerr. I don't see how we can stop it. I'm waiting for one of those—' he motioned towards the papers irritably—'to come out with a flaring accusation against America, or Russia—anyone. When it comes there'll be a general demand for action and...'

Craigie stopped for a moment, and drew a deep breath. Then he went on more incisively:

'But talking like this is nonsense. I drummed it into the Cabinet last night, before poor Garney went; you don't need telling. We've got to find Marlin and Kelly. I've called a dozen men and they're waiting any time you like, Kerr. But first, what happened up in the North?'

Kerr explained, briefly. Craigie nodded, and was not surprised by his agent's final:

'Have you the list of Marlin's clients handy?'

Craigie had. Kerr took another sheet of paper from his pocket and compared the two. The second list was that supplied by Mrs. Trentham of Jeremy Potter's regular callers: Not until they reached the 'M' sections did Kerr see what he wanted, and then his eyes glinted.

'Mayhew,' he snapped. 'There's our man, all right. He quarrelled with Potter, he's taken a lot of trouble to cover his movements, and he's on both lists. His address on this—' he waved the list of Marlin's clients—'is the Lucretia Hotel, Bayswater. A call there might help. I think I'll go myself.'

'I should,' Craigie agreed. Now he was dealing with the more routine work of the Department, he seemed more like his usual self. 'And there's another man you might look up, Kerr. Potter's brother.'

'And Potter's niece,' Kerr added grimly. 'I telephoned from Heston to have that young lady watched. Miller said he'd look after it. What stopped Miller from coming north last night?'

'I decided to keep him here,' said Craigie slowly. 'He's more useful in London; he knows it better.'

Kerr nodded, and smiled wryly as he stood up:

'And Timothy?'

'I sent him to Pockham, to replace Trale.'

'Good,' said Kerr. 'Well, Davidson and I ought to be able to tackle the Lucretia and Miss Smith, although if we could have a man or two following us, in case of emergency, it would help.'

'Go to the Carilon,' said Craigie, 'ask for Carruthers and a man named Beaumont; they'll be all right. Carruthers knows you, so there won't be any difficulty. Telephone me if anything at all develops, and don't take any chances.'

'What are chances?' asked Bob Kerr gently.

Craigie felt better when the two men had left. There was something comforting in the way Kerr approached the situation. Craigie told himself he had never known a man who took things so calmly, or was less likely to be knocked off-balance. It was a refreshing thought that Kerr was working with the Department, and it made up a little for the general grimness of the situation.

That was bad. Craigie had said no more than the truth on the previous night when he had told the assembled Cabinet that the country was seething, and the morning's papers made the position much more grave. Over London—and over England—there was a poorly suppressed excitement; the country knew that it was only a matter of time, now, before war broke out.

And Craigie knew every eye was directed towards Russia.

The squalling of the Fascist press in Germany and Italy and the mid-European states, was stronger than ever. England, according to these, was at long last suffering from the results of its tendency to sympathise with the Soviet regime: unless England was careful, it would fall under the heel of the Soviet and—the identical statement recurred again and again—if that happened, Fascism would unite to 'combat the terror'.

The international complications worried Craigie. He waited anxiously for the first wireless reports to come from the States, ready any moment to hear that a similar outrage had occurred over there. The trouble was that it seemed impossible to predict where the flare-up would start. It might—and he was inclined to believe this, although he knew that on the surface of it the idea was absurd—come between Britain and America; on the other hand the dictator-countries' outcry against Russia might force Britain's hand against the Soviet. And there were other possibilities...

Well, thought Craigie, it had been coming long enough, and there had been ample warnings. He ran over them slowly, in his mind. Starting from the absurdity of the Locarno Pact and the natural—the inevitable—secession of Germany from it, a hundred straws had shown the direction of the wind. The meteoric rise of Hitler, the gradual combination of the Italo-Germanic pact, the increasing number of countries with Fascist regimes yoked together under the term 'Mid-European', the natural strengthening of the armaments position of those few countries with more democratic sympathies, the inevitable re-arming everywhere—all these things had told him, and should have told the others. But there was madness in some countries, and blindness in others.

He reflected wearily on the appalling examples the world had seen in recent years.

The Italian crushing of Abyssinia, the inhuman fight between the military and the democrats in Spain; the Portuguese rebellions—following each other so swiftly that sooner or later the ruling Government must fall; the European uprising against Jewry—with its like in Palestine, where Britain was still trying without success to crush the revolt; Hitler's heavy arms programme and the re-militarising of the Rhine zone: the Moscow Trial, indicative of the unrest in the Soviet and—perhaps worse than any of the others, although not fully appreciated anywhere—the bitterness that was growing apace among the black races, against the racial distinction, which Hitler and the other Fascist powers were driving hard. All these things spelled only one thing together— WAR. It *must* come.

And there were other things. Japan, after her shock when she had tried to raid Europe and had failed—when Burke had performed what was almost a miracle—was still ready to pounce on Western weakness. Craigie knew—and that was the reason why he was more worried than he had ever been in his life—that once the flare came, it would be world-wide.

The immediate cause of the war-fever, the sabotage and outrages organised by Marlin, must be eliminated if there was to be breathing space before the conflagration. If it could be eliminated, the rumblings on the Continent might yet die down... *if*...

Craigie sighed, tapped out his pipe in the fireplace, stood up and walked to his desk. He took out the map of England, with its marked locations of military and other bases, and studied it for a long time.

11

MRS. TRENTHAM TALKS

Carruthers and Beaumont were waiting at the Carilon for Kerr and Davidson, who had gone to the Lucretia Hotel ahead of the others. Kerr, with the habit of years, was able to forget the issues at stake and to concentrate exclusively on the matter of immediate concern. He wanted to find the man Mayhew, and he was convinced that if he could do so, he would be very near to finding Marlin.

The Manager of the Lucretia—one of the smaller, Victorian-style hotels—was a mild-mannered man of close to seventy. He was pleased to offer all the help he could to these special police agents, as Kerr and Davidson called themselves.

'A Mr. Mayhew? Yes, he had had a Mr. Mayhew staying for a few weeks. That would have been immediately after Christmas...

'Was he a tall man, Mr. Williams?' Kerr asked.

'No—only about five-nine, I should say. He had rather a stoop—nothing exaggerated, but there.'

'Did he wear glasses?'

'Oh, yes. Those very thick, horn-rimmed ones.'

'I see,' said Kerr, grimly. He had a mental picture of this man Mayhew, walking with a stoop deliberately to hide his true height, wearing glasses to hide his eyes and—with their thick horn rims—his eyebrows. 'How did he dress, Mr. Williams?'

'Oh, very well, sir. He was most particular about his clothes. He invariably wore dark grey.'

Another unobtrusive factor, Kerr noted bleakly. Then the manager added:

'Oh, one thing I quite forgot, Mr. Kerr. He had a limp; a pronounced limp, on the right side. He threw his leg forward a little—you know how I mean?'

'Indeed I do,' said Kerr, his eyes gleaming. 'Now, if you can tell me just when he first came here, and how often he visited the hotel...?'

Williams turned up his records, which showed that Mayhew had first stayed at the Lucretia for a week immediately after Christmas: he had gone away for five days and returned for two weeks, gone again for ten days, then returned for a final week. When he left, it was reportedly for a longish trip abroad.

'Did he have any visitors, Mr. Williams?'

'One man did come once or twice, I know sir, But I didn't see him myself; my assistant mentioned it.'

'Can I see the assistant?' asked Kerr.

He could; and five minutes later, had more reason than ever to know that Mayhew was his man. For the caller—who had given his name as Smith—had been tall, scholarly-looking, and with a peculiarly sallow skin. Kerr had not seen Marlin, but he knew the description fitted well enough.

It was impossible, unfortunately, to ascertain the actual dates on which 'Smith' had called at the Lucretia; Kerr gave up trying, and pressed for still more information about his visitors. There had been one or two who had called briefly, it seemed, but the assistant manager and the reception clerk had no clear memory of them.

Kerr described what he could of the man he knew as Kelly; but the instigator of the Pockham outrage had not, so far as the Lucretia management knew, visited the mysterious Mr. Mayhew. Disappointed, Kerr prepared to go.

'No lady visitors, I suppose?' he added idly.

'Only on two occasions, sir, when he had a secretary call here. I forget the woman's name. A Mrs. Trenchard, or Trentham, or—sir! Is there something wrong?'

Without a word, Kerr had reached for the telephone.

'Trunks?' he was saying now. 'Get me Preston 09317. Official business, please.'

Craigie had told him that once the Cabinet had realised the real danger of the situation, all telephone exchanges had been instructed that the words 'official business' were to earn callers immediate priority, and he was certainly connected with The Larches in record time.

'Trale?' he asked, recognising the voice.

'Yes,' said Dodo. He recognised Kerr, too, but automatically following the ritual Craigie insisted his Department men use in telephoning each other, he spelt his name backwards.

Kerr followed suit, then added quickly:

'Is Mrs. Trentham still there?'

His relief when Trale said 'Yes' was enormous.

'Fine! Don't let her out of your sight—let her go out if she wants to, but follow her yourself. That woman's not all she seems. Don't lose her, or you'll lose your neck! I'll come up right away.'

'By air?'

'How else?'

'All right, all right!' Trale laughed wryly. He was a good

Department man—one of the best—and no-one had Craigie's interests more at heart. But his supreme imperturbability was not matched by an ability to think and act on the instant. On the other hand, he had yet to fail in any job he was given, and he was a match for most men with fists or gun.

'I'll be waiting, Bob,' he promised.

'Good man,' said Kerr, and rang off.

Williams was obviously a little breathless to find himself caught up in such dramatic happenings, and clearly impressed by the famous flier's abrupt but casual:

'Another trip, Wally. Call Heston, will you, and tell them to have that bus ready? Now, Mr. Williams—before we go: you can't tell me of any other visitors?'

'None at all, to my knowledge, sir.'

'And nothing that might help us to locate Mr. Mayhew?'

'I'm so sorry—I have no idea at all where he was going.'

Kerr smiled mechanically, his mind already darting elsewhere.

'Thank you, Mr. Williams—I may telephone you a little later in the day. Good morning.'

The two men reached Preston in something under two hours, and entered the porch of Jeremy Potter's house at an interesting moment. For Mrs. Trentham was about to enter the drive.

They had left the airfield by car, and Kerr had seen the woman, with Trale following unobtrusively behind, walking sharply up the Lancaster Road.

He was in the hall before the others, and when Mrs. Trentham entered, he smiled and bowed. Davidson followed suit, remarking that it was a nice day—and Mrs. Trentham gravely agreed, then she excused herself to go to her room. She was dressed in black, Kerr noticed, and the quiet clothing gave her a prettiness she had not possessed when he had last seen her. She seemed more self-assured now, despite her outward display of mourning, and Kerr wondered what she would say when he asked how often she had visited London—and Mr. Mayhew.

Before he questioned her, however, he wanted to talk with Trale; he was curious as to that morning's walk;

Trale couldn't be sure there was anything in it.

'She went to the North Country Bank,' he reported, 'and then to a hairdresser's—funny how these women put hair before anything else. Stayed there about an hour, and walked straight back here. That's the lot. I have the addresses, in case you want 'em.'

'I might,' said Kerr. 'It wouldn't be a bad idea if you inquired at that hairdresser's right away.'

'Telephone, you mean?'

'Go and see them,' Kerr advised. Adding, as Dodo seemed about to protest: 'We've got to try everything, Trale. *Everything.* Timothy'd better go with you.'

'Sorry, sergeant!' Dodo grinned, sketching a mock salute. 'So long.'

He went out with Timothy Arran, and Kerr smiled as he looked at his watch. It was half-past two, which explained why he was feeling hungry. Now he came to think of it, he hadn't had much in the way of breakfast. Nor had Davidson, who offered to go and see what he could persuade Oakwood to rustle up.

'I suppose,' he added, 'you don't think it wise to leave Mrs. T. for a few hours? She might pay some more rewarding visits, while if you talk to her she'll be wise to the trouble and stay at home.'

'I can't lose time,' Kerr objected.

'Well, good luck!' said Wally philosophically. 'If you feel as hungry as I do, you'll hope she won't keep you too long.'

Kerr nodded wryly, and turned towards the stairs. He knew where Mrs. Trentham's room was, and wondered what her reaction would be.

Her 'come in', in answer to his knock, was cool enough. But he obeyed, and closed the door behind him. Mrs. Trentham was sitting at a desk, an accounts book open before her. She was particularly well-groomed, and even a less observant man than Kerr could have seen that her hair had recently been dressed.

'Hope I'm not butting in?' he enquired, with his widest smile. Perhaps it was the knowledge that she could have told him a great deal more than she had about the mysterious Mr. Mayhew, that made him think she looked more capable, this morning, and—although the word was absurd—dangerous. There was a sharp glint in her eyes he could not fathom.

'There's a lot to do,' said Mrs. Trentham, 'and I don't think I ought to stop because—well...'

'I know.' Kerr had a sudden vision of Jeremy Potter, lying outstretched on the hearth-rug with that dreadful circle of crimson around his neck, and reminded himself of the woman's terror—which he was sure *had* been genuine. He did not believe anyone could have acted as convincingly as that. 'Mr. Potter's solicitors have been along, I take it?'

'Yes; but only for a few minutes. Is there anything I can do for you?'

She glanced at the book pointedly, as if to say that if Kerr wanted no more than a few minutes' idle conversation, she wished he would go elsewhere for it. He smiled again, answering her:

'Yes, there's one little thing: Why didn't you tell me you had been to see Mr. Mayhew at the Lucretia Hotel, Mrs. Trentham?'

He had spoken as easily and lightly, as though enquiring about her general well-being. But as he finished, she was staring at him—with something of the previous night's horror in her eyes. Her whole body was rigid, and for a full minute after he had stopped, she couldn't speak. Kerr watched her closely, and with deep satisfaction: he was on to a warm trail, at last.

'But—but,' Kerr's voice hardened.

'It's useless to say you didn't. I've been busy, Mrs. Trentham, and I know a great deal. Particularly, that you lied last night when you told me you didn't know Mayhew well. That looks suspiciously as though you have reason to wish to shield him.'

She was still staring at him, but made an effort to answer rationally.

'I—I don't know what to say.' She was very pale now, and again Kerr noted how her looks suffered when she was under stress of emotion.

'I think,' he said grimly, 'you'd better tell me all you know about the man, without further prevarication.'

He was standing between her and the door: solid, impassive—a man who clearly could and probably would go to any length to make her talk—and in sudden panic, she pushed her chair back from the desk.

'I can't tell you! Mr. Potter sent me to London to take notes and he made me swear I'd never talk...'

'Don't lie,' Kerr snapped. 'I want the truth.'

'I'm giving it!' She was almost wild with alarm now. 'You can't make me tell what I don't know!'

'I can make you tell what you *do* know.' His eyes bored into hers. 'I think you had better change your mind, Mrs. Trentham.'

'I can't, I tell you! Oh, I can't stand this! What are you trying to do; what are you trying to say? You've no right to ask questions without someone else here, you...'

'I think,' said Kerr, in a dangerously quiet voice, 'you'd better get this straight, Mrs. Trentham. You may or may not know that Mr. Potter's murder is incidental to a larger inquiry, and that the situation is serious enough for us to forget that there is a law in this country to protect the accused...'

'I'm not accused of anything! How dare you say I am?'

'Whether they are innocent or guilty,' Kerr went on, as though she had not interrupted. 'There are police downstairs, and they have had instructions to close their ears to anything they might hear from this room. There is no limit, Mrs. Trentham, to the methods of persuasion I can use. I don't want to use them, but I must know all you know of the man Mayhew. Now—are you going to talk?'

He saw the increasing horror in her eyes, and he hated his job more than he could have said. After all, she was probably mixed up in this business without knowing quite why. On the other hand, she *knew* something about Mayhew; might even be able to tell him what the man was doing and where he was.

And suddenly Bob Kerr realised the importance of Mayhew in the mystery of the sabotage.

He was amazed that he had not seen it before—and that Craigie had missed it, too. Because Mayhew was known to have travelled from one country to another. Mayhew was probably the travelling agent for Marlin...

'Come on, *talk!*' he commanded, harshly. 'I'll give you two minutes.' He had a sudden sharp awareness of what this whole thing meant: a sudden memory of that explosion at Pockham, and all its victims. '*Talk,* damn you!'

'No, no!' she almost screamed. 'I don't know anything— how could...'

Kerr took one step forward. His right hand closed around her forearm, hard enough to make her wince.

'Don't be a fool,' he warned.

He wasn't prepared for what came. With one jerk, she had wrenched her arm away and jumped from her chair, pulling her bag off the desk. More quickly than he would have credited, she had a gun out and was standing by the window, glaring fanatically at him, the gun trembling in her shaking fingers—but pointing straight at his chest.

Robert McMillan Kerr had often been surprised, but never had he been taken so completely off his guard. For a moment, he stared at the gun almost stupidly. Then he looked up, into the woman's eyes.

'As bad as that, is it?' he said gently—then sprang sideways. There was a stab of yellow flame and the sharp *zutt*! of a silenced automatic—but even before the bullet had hit the door, Kerr had kicked out with his right leg: this was no time for niceties. He caught her ankle and she cried aloud in pain and alarm as she staggered, the gun dropping from her fingers.

Kerr swooped on it, then stood up slowly.

'That didn't work exactly to plan,' he remarked conversationally, and if his expression had frightened her before, it seemed to terrify her, now.

She was breathing quickly, her breast heaving. Her eyes *did* not leave his for a moment.

Then suddenly, ridiculously, she demanded: 'Well, what are you going to do, now?' Her voice was high, artificial: 'You —beast!'

Kerr almost laughed. It was an act, and a poor one. She was putting on a show. For whatever reason, she was playing for time.

'Come along, Mrs. Trentham—don't drag it out any more. I shall have to...'

'How dare you cross-question me like this! Who do you think you are? *Get out of my room!*' she screamed, suddenly. 'Get *out*! If Mr. Potter knew you were pestering me—'

'Wally!' he shouted, over his shoulder. 'Come up, will you?'

Davidson raced up the stairs. He had been waiting at the foot of them, curious as to what her hysterical shouting might connote. As he reached the landing, Kerr called:

'See if you can find a dog-whip—or a length of rope. This fool thinks she's clever.'

Wally grinned. 'There's a thing in the hall—a long thing—'

'I remember,' said Kerr. 'Just what I want. Tell Moor to ignore her shouting, will you?'

'Leave it to me!' Davidson almost fell down the stairs with laughter. For Kerr to speak of whipping a woman—!

He reached the hall, still chuckling, and took the whip—an ornamental silver-mounted one—from its bracket in the wall. He cracked it once, and turned towards the stairs.

It was then that the front door opened. Wally hardly realised that was strange, for a moment. He should have done, for he had heard Moor give instructions that no one was to enter with a key. Oakwood had, indeed, surrendered all the keys on the previous evening. But the door was opened with one—and as he saw the three men in the porch, he realised it was all wrong. His hand dropped to his pocket, but he was a fraction of a second too late.

The florid-faced, bushy-moustached man who entered first was smiling unpleasantly. His hand came from his pocket quickly, revealing his gun, as he stepped into the hall. He was followed by two men, the last one closing the door behind him.

As Wally stood staring unbelievingly, the florid-faced man laughed.

'Seen a ghost, Davidson?' He chuckled again. 'If you haven't, you soon will do. Where's the woman?'

Davidson's eyes were very narrow: he needed no telling of the danger. He still could hardly credit the fact that 'Kelly' was here: the man who had been at Pockham—the man who had shot Toby Arran. The florid-faced man could be no-one else. The description fitted too perfectly.

Benson, sometimes known as Kelly—glared as Wally made no answer. He took two steps forward before the Department man could guess what was coming, and hacked viciously at his shins.

'Talk, you blasted fool! Where's Trentham?'

Wally Davidson was a man who looked tired—and often was—but who had never failed to give a good account of himself when it came to action. A split second before, he had been wondering what had happened to Inspector Moor and the three policemen still in the house; and the servants. The mystery baffled him, and he was already on edge.

As Benson's toe-cap cracked into his shin, he saw red. And if the intruders had never seen a fighting-machine before, they saw one now.

The startling abruptness of it, the apparent madness of it— for Davidson could have been drilled half-a-dozen times in the first ten seconds—did more to help him than anything else. His first punch caught Benson full on the nose, so that he staggered back, tears streaming down his face. Davidson, his own face very white, smashed home two more punches—this time, to the stomach—to send a now unconscious Benson cannoning into the men behind him, neither of whom had dared shoot before because his back was towards them. Davidson swept on as though they were half his size. It was devastation. He sent one man crashing into the wall and the other sprawling on the floor, then went after the man against the wall and hit him three times, viciously, in the face. The man's lips split as the blood welled up, but Davidson ignored his now lacerated knuckles and simply turned to the man on the floor.

The man on the floor raised his gun.

Davidson dodged the first bullet, but he had no time to prevent a second. The man touched the trigger—and for a moment Davidson thought it was the end. But before the bullet left the gun, something pecked into the man's back. He groaned and started, and the bullet went wide. A second something pecked into his leg and he rolled over and over on the floor cursing, and shouting.

Davidson, standing very still and staring upwards, felt the red mist clear from his eyes.

'Hello, Kerr,' he said absurdly.

'Busy?' asked Bob Kerr, starting down the stairs, gun in hand. 'Now I know why that little vixen's been stalling. She's been waiting for this. I think...'

What Kerr thought at that moment was never recorded, for sharply across his words came the voice of another man. It came from the rear of the house—and fast upon it, the hurrying footsteps of several men.

'I'm clear, Benson! Are you?'

Naturally, there was no answer. As naturally, Davidson reached for his gun. But before he touched it, Kerr snapped:

'Upstairs, man!'

Davidson hesitated for a fraction of a second. As he did so, the door to the servants' quarters opened wide, and on the threshold he saw three men—or possibly four. He also saw a tommy-gun in the first man's hands, and leapt for the stairs. There was a volley of curses, then, suddenly and wickedly, the rat-tat-tat of the machine-gun's bullets hitting the front door.

Davidson always swore that Kerr's second sense must have warned him what was coming; certainly if they had been together in the hall, nothing would have saved them from the fusillade. He was at the head of the stairs by the time Kerr reached Mrs. Trentham's door, and glanced over his shoulder. He saw the gunman skidding round the banisters so as to re-aim—and ducking, he raced for the door Kerr had entered.

In the room, Bob Kerr was reaching for the telephone with one hand, while Mrs. Trentham—that quiet, supposedly terri-fied little woman—was fighting like a wildcat to prevent him. Wally was in time to see her fasten her teeth into Kerr's free hand—but she broke away as she saw him, and rushed for the door. He swung aside at the right moment and, without hesi-tation, swept her legs from under her. As she crashed down, screaming, there was the thunder of footsteps on the stairs.

It was bedlam.

Kerr was shouting into the telephone to make himself heard, the woman was screaming like a maniac, the footsteps were now clattering along the hall within yards of the door, and the machine-gun was providing a steady barrage clearly designed to prevent anyone coming out. Davidson kicked the door shut—and a split second later, the bullets were pecking into it.

'*Damn* that woman!' he swore fervently. And as if echoing the sentiment, Kerr banged down the telephone, strode across to the still screaming Mrs. Trentham, and yanked her to her feet. Her shrieks seemed to couple in intensity—from fear, or rage, or both—and he did the only thing he could.

A sharp rap to her chin knocked her unconscious and he

let her drop with a thud as he sprang towards the desk. Davidson followed intuitively—and only later he had time to marvel at the speed of it all, as together they crashed the hefty desk against the door at the very moment it opened and the snout of the machine-gun was jammed through.

'Keep clear of that,' Kerr murmured matter-of-factly, and Wally gave a wry grin as the flames stabbed viciously through the two-inch gap, the bullets ripping a line of holes in the opposite wall.

Again in unspoken agreement, they turned to the only other piece of furniture that could help them: a seven-foot high, solid mahogany cupboard. Luckily, it was only bracketed to the wall and they wrenched it away with one heave.

'Let it drop,' Kerr advised.

It fell with a resounding crash, and the pictures in the room were still swaying as they lugged it across and jammed it hard between the wall at one end and the desk at the other. By this time, the door was some four or *five* inches open but at least not wide enough for a man to squeeze through.

For the first time since he had heard Davidson scrapping in the hall, Kerr relaxed. And Wally almost laughed aloud as he calmly proffered cigarettes with the comment:

'Bit close, what?'

'Close!' Davidson echoed, accepting automatically. 'I've never struck anything so ruddy warm in my life! What the hell are we going to do? What the devil has happened?'

'Caught by that.' Kerr gestured towards the inert figure on the floor. 'She must have telephone the moment she got in here.' He grimaced sourly. 'Her friend—Kelly, by the look of him—has obviously got at least half a dozen men with him. God knows what's happened to Moor, but I'm glad Trale's still at large. Kelly,' he added thoughtfully, 'is the most direct man I've ever met.'

'I could show you another,' grinned Davidson.

He was amazed. Here was Kerr, discussing the thing coolly over a cigarette—and there were the gunmen still firing into the room, still thudding against the door. They would soon realise the barricade was too strong, but that didn't prevent Davidson from realising that things could still go wrong at any moment. The possibility had not, apparently, occurred to Kerr.

'We're all right,' Kerr said, as if guessing his thoughts. 'I told the Preston police and they'll be here in ten minutes or less. But it's probably hoping too much, to suppose these fellows won't have the wit to suspect it. If they...'

He broke off at the sudden cessation of the din outside. Then through the silence, they heard Benson urge:

'That's enough! Get clear while you can.'

Davidson looked at Kerr, who shrugged wryly.

'So they're going—ah, well! We can't stop them. We'd be cut to ribbons if we tried to show our noses. We've got her—' he nodded grimly at the still unconscious figure—'and I daresay she can be made to talk. Although I'm not sure she's sane. I've thought all along there must be someone mad behind this business, and she's a start. Well...'

He shrugged again, then crossed to the window, taking out his gun as he went. Keeping well to one side, he peered out— and cursed as he realised that this was the rear of the house and he could see nothing of the front, nor of the road beyond. As he glanced around the grounds, he knew that with three or four men, he could have made some sort of a fight. But the odds were hopeless, now, and wishing would not alter them.

12

MARK POTTER'S VERSION

There were twenty armed policemen in the five black cars which arrived from Preston exactly twelve minutes after Kerr and Davidson had barricaded themselves in. They found none of the gunmen on the premises—but they did find other things.

Inspector Moor, shot three times through the chest and mortally wounded, was in the kitchen, where he had been talking with Oakwood. The butler had been cracked over the head but not shot—obviously the attackers had not considered him much danger. The five women-servants were crammed together in a locked pantry, four of them barely conscious by the time a policeman opened the door to have the nearest fall out at his feet. The other three menservants were missing.

Kerr swore as he guessed why: they must have been expecting Kelly to arrive—as that woman had. Obviously, they had gone with him.

'Of course,' Davidson suggested, 'they might have been forced?'

Kerr shook his head: 'He'd have shot them out of hand, if

they'd been in his way. They must have been his own men, working with—or against—Potter. We've a lot to learn about Potter yet.'

'If they were Kelly's men,' objected Davidson, 'why did they stay here as long as they did?'

Kerr laughed, without humour.

'Because they weren't worried about the police; the police would inquire about the murder, and that was normal enough. They were waiting for us to return: as soon as we did, their boss was told and he came for us. Kelly obviously doesn't like Craigie's men.'

His theories were not far wrong. Benson was indeed concerned with Craigie's men. He—and Marlin, at Putney, where he had been informed by telephone—had been shocked by Kerr's appearance at The Larches. They could have understood it had he arrived after the Potter murder was known: they were baffled by his arrival sooner—and very glad that Jeremy Potter was dead. He might have told Kerr a great deal...

Kerr telephoned a brief but full report to Craigie, and was told to carry on in the north while there seemed any chance of getting a clue. There must be a great deal of information somewhere in that area, he reasoned—if only they could find it. Of the Trentham woman, Craigie said:

'Make her talk, Kerr. Don't have any qualms, make her talk as you'd make Kelly talk, if necessary.'

'I'll try,' said Kerr. 'But if she really is unbalanced, we'll be out of luck.'

'Handle it as you deem best,' Craigie told him, and Kerr grunted dry acceptance as he replaced the receiver.

Davidson, now back to his usual form, had managed to

find a crate of beer. Reaction to the whole affair had caught up with Oakwood, who was now dazed and in a state of shock, and none of the women servants was in any state to prepare a meal. So the two Department men helped themselves to the beer, cold meat and bread.

Their hunger was at least checked, if hardly satisfied, when some minutes later a police-sergeant brought them news of a visitor: Mark Potter, brother of the late Jeremy.

Mark Potter proved to be a man of medium height, autocratic manner, and grim determination. His suit and high cravat might have suggested an era far removed from the present day, but he carried his silver-knobbed walking-stick as if he would use it without a qualm if the need arose.

'And who are you, sir,' he demanded stridently, as Kerr appeared, 'to keep me waiting in the hall of my own house? It's an impertinence, sir—it's outrageous!'

'I am so sorry.' Kerr was at his most ingratiating. 'But—well, sir, the circumstances are somewhat unusual. I...'

'Unusual! My brother is murdered and you can find no better word than that! I wish,' said Potter bitterly, 'I had hurried here immediately the news came through. I might have been able to take control. As it is...'

'Why didn't you come immediately?' asked Kerr, mildly.

'Because some interfering busybody at Scotland Yard requested that I wait in London!' snapped Potter.

Kerr smiled inwardly. Obviously Craigie had not wanted the investigations in Preston impeded, and had ensured that Mark Potter could not make himself a nuisance for a while, at least.

In the event, he was surprisingly easy to handle. The Preston Superintendent, Caldicott, helped matters along by letting him know just who Kerr was, and he clearly knew the famous airman by repute. He was quietened, too, by the news of the raid on the house, and the death of Inspector Moor: he seemed to suffer a bigger shock from that, indeed, than from his brother's death. The fact puzzled Kerr, who disliked mysteries, and he asked a pertinent question:

'Did you have any reason to believe your brother was in danger, Mr. Potter?'

The other's eyes narrowed, and he pursed his lips.

'Well... Not exactly danger, Mr. Kerr. I—er—my brother and I were not the best of friends, lately. I, as you probably know, handled the export orders of the Mills, and he was—er —in command here. I did not,' he elaborated, uncomfortably, 'approve of the way he carried out his business. This is a difficult thing for me to say, Mr. Kerr, for I held Jeremy in considerable regard. The fact remains that he was associated with certain people whom I heartily disliked.'

'Perhaps if I say,' suggested Kerr, 'that it is possible this investigation will be rather more far-reaching than the straightforward discovery of the murderer, you will feel more at ease?'

Mark Potter darted him an inquisitive glance.

'Yes—yes, I will. I hope later you will be able to amplify remarks that might be considered—er—ambiguous? But to proceed. The result of my brother's friendship with these men was that export orders were invariably late for delivery and had serious adverse results on profits; you will understand why I feel so strongly on the matter.'

Kerr did understand, and smiled to himself a little ruefully. He was even more rueful five minutes later, when he heard that the 'certain people' consisted of a group of industrial firms who, in Mark Potter's opinion, offered absurdly low prices for material. For the sake of formality, Kerr took their names and addresses—only to recognise them all as manufacturers of materials which had no connection with armaments.

But if Mark Potter had blown and then pricked one bubble, he had another to come.

'Of course, the Mid-European Entente's boycott on the import of manufactured cotton goods, last year, had a very serious effect on Jeremy. *I* suffered from the loss of a large annual turnover, but the thing seemed to make Jeremy bitter. Then Halloway left our board...'

Which Halloway?' demanded Kerr.

'Sir Kenneth, the present Under-Secretary for Defence. Of course, Halloway's father and ourselves were very good friends. Young Halloway—' Kerr smiled at the 'young'; Kenneth Halloway was nearly fifty—'was never a whole-hearted supporter. He much preferred politics. And as soon as our profits began to decline, he resigned.'

'Purely because of decline in profits?' Kerr could not see the Under-Secretary deserting a sinking ship.

'Well—to be honest, Mr. Kerr, I think Jeremy put his back up. A rough colloquialism, but in this case true. I seem,' added Potter a little awkwardly, 'to be painting a very black picture of my brother, and I have not the slightest desire to do so. But facts are facts.'

'Yes,' said Kerr, 'I appreciate that.'

He believed he appreciated other things, too. The Potter Mills, despite those Government contracts, were not flour-ishing as they should have been. Jeremy Potter had been accepting orders at low prices, and the loss of a substantial mid-European trade must have been a severe blow.

It did not seem too long a jump to assume that Jeremy had found himself losing money heavily, and has listened to Martin—or 'Kelly'—and agreed in some way to help in their campaign. It was not a far cry from that to the assumption that 'Kelly' and Potter had fallen out—but not before Jeremy's secretary and some of the servants had been bought over by Marlin—and Jeremy had died.

In some ways, perhaps, it had been as well for him.

'And now, if I may,' said Mark Potter, 'I'll go upstairs. There are doubtless a lot of things to be done and—' his voice hardened suddenly,—'the less that Trentham woman has to do with it, the better. I shall dismiss her.'

'Why?' asked Kerr, suddenly alert.

'Why? Good God, Kerr, there are a dozen reasons! She used to be Halloway's secretary, until he dismissed her. I can never understand Jeremy employing her—he was a good Conservative, if nothing else. No amount of efficiency,' added Mark Potter emphatically, 'can compensate for blatant Communism. And Mrs. Trentham has strong Red sympathies. She went to Russia for a holiday some years ago, and seemed a different woman when she returned.'

Kerr lost no time in telephoning Craigie. For the first time, there appeared to be a direct line leading from 'Kelly' to Russia —or at least to Communism. Was this to be a case of crying 'wolf once too often? Was this series of crimes in fact instigated by the Soviet Union? Or was there something even more subtle behind it?

Craigie could be no more certain of the answers than Kerr himself. But he did have one item of interest to impart: the man Kerr knew as 'Kelly' was in fact a close associate of Marlin's, by the name of Benson...

It was half-past three before the police gave up the hope of getting immediate information that would help locate the attackers. The Larches was a large house, standing back from the road—along which a great deal of traffic passed. There were several other houses near, but all of them were hidden by trees from the Potter drive.

Benson's car—or cars—had turned off the main road without being observed, and with the help of the men-servants, he must have had little trouble in overcoming the police in the house.

Davidson's arrival in the hall had coincided with that of Benson himself, and the men who made the frontal attack, for which Kerr and he were devoutly thankful. But for that, they would have been dead; there was no question of that.

'And if they hadn't been so anxious to locate Mrs. T.—' Wally shrugged expressively, and Kerr nodded.

'They were anxious to get her all right, and that's worth knowing. I'd like to make her talk—and,' he eyed Davidson grimly: 'I'd like to make Penelope Smith talk! I wonder where she is?'

'Ask me,' said Wally. 'Or better still, ask Tim.'

It was a question which Timothy Arran was asking himself, for he was a worried man. The more he thought of Penelope, the less he liked the idea that she was, even indirectly, mixed up in this game. And while he was at Pockham, trying to squeeze further information from Tippett and other inhabitants of that village of sorrow, he had plenty of time to brood.

For two days, nothing developed.

The demand for action in the daily Press grew more clamorous than ever, the degree of public unrest more fevered, and the efforts of the Government to keep the national calm—for the belief that the Pockham outrage had been a deliberate act of war, from a so far unknown foreign country, was now firmly accepted—grew more desperate. Craigie was summoned to this meeting and that, but he could report nothing definite. Mrs. Trentham recovered from her spell of unconsciousness but remained mute; she seemed to live in a daze, which five of the most celebrated mind-specialists in the country certified as a form of amnesia that nothing but time could overcome.

The Cabinet, naturally, had not been idle. Halloway, with his expert knowledge, and Sir James Cathie began a hurried tour of the large arsenals and munition factories. On the surface of it, nothing notable was revealed. Here and there, they were told, there had been attempts to spread sedition, but nothing stronger than the usual Communist efforts—with, as Halloway saw it, one important difference.

It was rare for American Communists to pay much attention to England; there was enough for them to do in the States. But by dint of questioning that would have done Craigie himself credit, Halloway discovered that five of the stump speakers near several of the arsenals had been American. Cathie was inclined to pooh-pooh the inference, but Halloway reported immediately to Wishart.

Wishart did not even tell his ministers, and officially only Cathie, Halloway, Craigie and Wishart knew of it. But on the second morning after Benson's attack on The Larches, the *Clarion* trumpeted a bald statement that American agents had joined forces with known Communist agitators, and demanded to know what the Government proposed to do about it. Before the Government had time to reply—if, indeed, it would have deigned to reply to the *Clarion*—the whole balance of affairs was shifted.

News came from America of the bombing of the heart of Chicago. Considerable damage was done, but the aeroplane concerned in the attack had escaped—and Craigie's lips tightened when he read the words 'in the direction of Canada'. Several people were badly hurt, but by a miracle, no one was killed. That fortunate fact did not temper the outpourings of the American press. Just as all colours had joined together in England after the Pockham disaster, so did every American daily lash its readers to a state of fury. And in every report, the significance of the flight towards Canada was emphasised.

The *New York Daily* said:

'It is inconceivable that the aeroplane which bombed Chicago came from the sea; and it could not have come from the Mexican border. It is not too much to claim that it came from Canada.

'The Daily *does not accuse the Canadian Government of complicity in or foreknowledge of the outrage, but it does believe that the machine and its occupants are now sheltering in Canada. It demands that representations be made to Ottawa and to London for the fullest search and investigation to be carried out. Failure to discover the perpetrators of the outrage is inconceivable,* if the Governments to which we have referred are serious in their efforts.'

Craigie and Wishart read the leader, wirelessed from America within minutes of publication, with growing anxiety —and no surprise when most of the American papers echoed its sentiments. It was typical of the state of national tension that most of the British and Canadian press took the attitude that America was unjustified in assuming the aeroplane had come from Canada (which obviously it had done) and that in all probability the raid had been engineered by someone in America itself.

As a result of this exchange of opinions, there was something of an exodus from both countries, Canadians and Englishmen and their families in the States left for home as quickly as possible. Every ship was packed, and Southampton seethed with returning Americans. And although there was no actual display of hostility, crowds gathered at the docks, silent and morose. Other crowds swarmed around the American Embassy in London, and American-owned factories throughout the country.

Then the vast Hyams Motor Corporation—American-owned—shut down, and shipped all its American employees back to the States. It was perhaps the most illconsidered action conceivable. Seven thousand British workmen were thrown out of work, and in the neighbourhood of the Hyams works, there began the first outward show of hostility towards the country, always considered Britain's staunchest friend— always looked on, indeed, as something more like a relative.

A Fascist newspaper took the opportunity of pointing out that since the American War of Independence, that country had nursed a grudge against Great Britain, and other organs of the daily Press—which should have known better—printed speeches from American politicians declaiming against the British Isles. The frenzied rhetoric of Big Bill Hopson, at whose outbursts the British had hitherto turned a deaf ear or a smile, now only further inflamed public opinion.

Philip Fenway, the American Ambassador to London, was friendly towards Great Britain for many reasons, his English wife not being one of them. He was perturbed by the threat of trouble but he refused to be panicked, and he did more to steady opinion in America than anyone else. In a time of madness Fenway was sane.

His Embassy had been the scene of several hostile demonstrations; as a consequence, he rarely travelled without a guard. His wife, in fact, protested when he went out at all: but she was of a protesting nature. She would have disliked it much more had she known where he was heading when he slipped out of the Embassy by a rear exit one night, about a week after the Chicago bombing. She herself was visiting friends at the time: Fenway had excused himself on the grounds of pressure of work.

Some fifty minutes later, he entered a flat overlooking the Thames at Putney. The girl who welcomed him was young, and even a confirmed woman-hater would have admitted her beauty. More, she was American. Fenway's wife—the daughter of an English peer—was constantly reminding him that he had held a very unimportant post when they first married, and that he owed most of his advancement to her connections. The truth of these reminders did nothing to make Fenway stop wishing he had married for love and accepted a minor position.

He left the Putney Mansions, three hours after he had arrived, a much happier man; and the girl did not know she would never see him again...

Fenway's decision to drive across Barnes Common, in order to prepare himself for the return to bondage, helped Benson's men a great deal. His own car was forced into the kerb on a Common road—and before he realised what was happening, the driver of the other had him out of it, with an automatic in his ribs.

'We want a talk with you,' said this worthy, gruffly.

'You can keep wanting,' snapped Fenway.

His words and his fist moved at the same time, but before the fist contacted he had been knocked unconscious from behind. His car was left at a nearby garage by a man the sleepy attendant did not see properly, and Fenway himself—bound and gagged, although still unconscious—was in the rear of a Daimler saloon, which he did not see at all.

Nine days after the affair at Preston, in which time Kerr and the others had followed trail after trail without headway, Craigie and Wishart met—unusually, at the office of Department Z. They did not know it was the evening of Fenway's adventure.

'I wanted to see you alone,' Wishart said. 'Craigie, you must get something done. This agitation is dreadful.'

'It's about what I told you to expect,' Craigie reminded him, soberly. 'When are you going to crack down on the Press?'

'When they do the same over there.'

Craigie smiled dourly.

'You'll have to wait a long time, the way their politics and Press are run. How are diplomatic relations?'

'Strained,' said Wishart simply. 'If it weren't for Fenway, they'd be very much worse.'

'As bad as that, eh? Well, we seem to have succeeded in stopping any more outrages over here. But if there's anything else in America, the effect will be the same.'

'But it's so absurd! None of us *wants* war!'

'Just for once,' Craigie said, 'the people do. Oh, they don't want it in so many words, but they want something to happen. The Hyams business started it. Now, there's hardly an American factory in this country still working. That means the big business interests over there are beginning to complain, and they control the Press. Our Press is shouting because American vested interests have shut hundreds of thousands of men out of work. The value of the pound has dropped lower than ever before, and the dollar's as bad over here.'

Wishart nodded; he had aged ten years in the past two weeks, and his voice was almost querulous.

'You could tackle the Press,' Craigie told him. 'Force them to adopt a friendly tone towards America—although I'm inclined to think that's too late. You'd have...'

He reached for the telephone at its second ring. 'Excuse me?'

Wishart inclined his head, and watching the Chief of British Intelligence take the call, saw his jaw tighten suddenly as he said: 'Hold on a moment.'

Lowering the receiver, Craigie drew a deep breath.

'It's Kerr,' he reported. 'He's found a trail and followed it. I'm afraid it's breaking-point, David.'

Wishart's colour ebbed.

What—?'

'Fenway,' said Craigie, flatly. 'Murdered.'

As Kerr returned from making his call, Horace Miller and Timothy Arran surveyed him questioningly across the outstretched body of the American Ambassador.

'Craigie says to keep it close,' he told them, drily. 'Not a word to a soul.'

It was easy to say; it might be easy to do, up to a point. But all three knew that the thing must come to light eventually, and wondered whether it would not have a worse effect if the Government hushed the thing up.

13

KERR IS SUSPICIOUS

The events of the past three hours flashed through Kerr's mind as he stood propped against the wall, staring blankly ahead of him. Whatever course was taken, the result of this thing would be unspeakable.

Five hours before, Lilian Trentham—who was under close observation at a West End Nursing Home—had suffered a bout of hysteria, in which she had mentioned the name Mayhew and a place called Crayshaw. The information had been passed to Scotland Yard, and Miller had immediately contacted Kerr, who was staying for a brief spell at the Arrans' flat with Timothy.

By the time Kerr and Arran had reached the Yard, Miller had located nine villages or towns in England and Scotland named Crayshaw, and a daunting list of houses bearing that name. Kerr had instinctively ignored the houses and sent Trale and Davidson to the Midlands and north to check the three Crayshaws there. Arran, Miller and Kerr himself had started on three within a fifty miles radius of London, driving in Timothy's Frazer Nash.

Their first two had drawn blanks. Dusk was falling as they approached the third, a village in Sussex, and drove up the narrow High Street.

'Small place,' Miller commented. 'We shan't be long here before we know whether we've any luck... Wonder where the local man lives?'

The local policeman was a man of unexpected preciseness and common-sense. There were only two newcomers to the neighbourhood: and a man who had recently bought the Priory, an old house about a mile from the village. Pucker, the constable, described him succinctly.

'Brick-red face, moustache, and...'

'Get on the running-board,' ordered Miller, 'and take us to the Priory. Hurry, man!'

Fifteen minutes later, the policeman helped the other three break down the door at the rear of the house. Five minutes later, in an upstairs room, they found the body of the American Ambassador. Fenway had been strangled; three hours earlier, at most.

'Late again,' Kerr said bitterly, as he went to telephone Craigie...

'There'll be hell to pay, when this gets out,' he added, now. 'Aren't we doing well? No motive: why should anyone but a damn fool want to set us at America's throat? No Marlin. No Benson. No Mayhew, and that reminds me, Timothy—when did you last see Penelope Smith?'

Timothy coloured.

'The day before yesterday,' he said. 'Of course, she's been up in Preston for a while. Mrs. Potter came straight back from Cannes when she heard the news, and Penelope has been with her most of the time since. She's in London, now, though.'

'Still following you?'

'I say, old boy, draw it mild! She was honest, anyhow.'

'I know,' said Kerr, 'I know. But I can't get rid of the idea that there was a connection somewhere between her arrival in London and the start of hostilities. Have you talked to her much about this business?'

'Not a great deal.'

'Did she know Mayhew?'

'No—at least, she says she didn't.'

'Don't tell me you actually permit yourself to doubt?' Kerr grinned. 'That's my boy. Now—how do I arrange a little chat with her?'

'If you keep a civil tongue in your head,' Timothy said, 'I'll arrange it for you.'

Kerr grinned again, then told him: 'Joking aside, Tim, I'd like another talk with her.'

Arran nodded, and Kerr turned to the Yard man, who had been making a telephone call of his own.

'Well, Miller, I'm leaving this nasty job to you. Tim had better come with me—all right?'

'I don't like it much,' admitted Miller wryly, 'but the men from Horsham will be here any minute, so not to worry.'

The men from Horsham arrived as Kerr and Arran left: two inspectors and two detective-sergeants only, as per Miller's instructions. Somehow the murdered man's identity had to be kept altogether secret for the time being.

Arran let Bob Kerr drive to London, and directed him to the hotel where Penelope was staying.

The Éclat was comparatively unaffected by the war scare: as the management said, it had to be. But as the Department men drove through the West End, the bawling of the newsboys filled their ears, and every placard they saw contained some reference to America. They passed several street-corner meetings being broken up by the police; and at Hyde Park saw a mass demonstration in progress. There was a grimness about it all that worried Kerr—but only, for the moment, as a side issue. He had long ago learned the valuable knack of concentrating exclusively on the job in hand, and he was doing so now...

Penelope was in the lounge, dressed for going out, and Kerr admitted that she looked ravishing. She saw them and smiled—she had forgiven Timothy for his outburst at Dover. She had not altogether overcome her dislike of Bob Kerr, however, although as he approached—with that unexpected smile that lightened his face so remarkably—she sensed the quality in him that had made him so immediately popular with the Department agents.

'Hello, there,' said Timothy. 'You know this fellow.'

'Only too well,' Penelope grimaced humorously, but gave Kerr her hand.

'I don't think we met under the right terms,' he said, taking it warmly. 'Tim, you keep quiet, or I'll sling you out. There are one or two things, Miss Smith, with which you may be able to help me.'

'Call her Penelope,' suggested Timothy. 'She quite likes it.'

'Perhaps Mr. Kerr doesn't,' said Penelope, quickly.

'Call him Bob,' said Tim ingenuously, 'and he will.'

Bob Kerr laughed, Penelope followed suit, and Timothy beamed to see the barrier between them broken down. He had learned to admire and respect Kerr, as well as like him—and Penelope he was fast learning to love.

'Now this man Mayhew,' Kerr was saying, shortly after, 'was a friend of your uncle's; yet no one seems to have known him well. It's a queer business, isn't it? Had you ever heard of him?'

'Only vaguely,' said Penelope. 'But then, Uncle didn't like to think I knew anything about his business affairs.'

Kerr's expression hardened.

'I'm very much afraid,' he told her, 'that there was good reason for that. He was—if appearances are anything to go by —mixed up with Marlin and Benson, and the footmen seem to have been part of Benson's flock.'

'Yes...' admitted Penelope grudgingly.

'And I can't get it out of my mind,' said Kerr, 'that there was more than a coincidence in your arrival in London and your assignment with the Arrans. I mean,' he eyed Penelope frankly: 'It's just possible your uncle knew the Arrans would be working against his—er—friend, and thought you would be able to look after them for a brief spell.'

Penelope reflected; Kerr had noticed before that she rarely spoke on the spur of the moment.

'But,' she objected, 'he knew I'd be going to France in twenty-four hours.'

'That's the rub,' admitted Kerr. 'Anyhow—you'd no inkling, before the morning you left Manchester, that you were going to be put in Timothy's care?'

'I certainly hadn't,' said Penelope, with such emphasis that Timothy chuckled.

'And no knowledge at all of Mayhew?' Kerr threw in again, casually. But Penelope seemed not to notice, and merely repeated that she had never seen Mayhew and had only vaguely heard of him.

'A pity,' said Kerr, 'A great pity. Well...'

He broke off as Penelope obviously caught sight of someone entering the hotel foyer, and turned to see the some-what pompous person of Mark Potter.

Potter looked an ageing man as he stumped across the lounge. His brow was furrowed, his eyes lacked lustre, and his old-fashioned dress had lost its immaculate appearance. Penelope could have told them that he had suffered much more from the notoriety that his brother's murder had brought on the business, than by his actual death.

'Are you ready, Penelope?' he demanded. He nodded frigidly to Arran, of whom he heartily disapproved, but thawed as he added: 'Well, Kerr—any developments?'

'Nothing useful, I'm afraid, sir.'

'A vile business; vile!' said Potter. 'You'll advise me, please, if there is anything at all I can do? I can't stop tonight—we are calling on Somerston, the company's legal adviser: an old family friend, of course. Ready, Penelope?'

'Yes, Uncle.' Penelope smiled at the others. 'I'll see you some time tomorrow, Tim.'

As the pair of them moved away, Kerr nodded towards the reception desk and murmured tensely: 'Watch that man, Tim!'

Timothy watched as the man signed the register and turned towards the lifts. He was limping a little on his right side—and Tim's memory clicked into gear.

'Williams' description of Mayhew?' he breathed.

'Good man!' said Kerr. 'After him, Tim.'

As Timothy disappeared unhesitatingly in the wake of the stranger, Bob Kerr moved casually towards the main doors...

Within five minutes, Timothy had seen the man with the limp enter room 87, had discovered from the attendant that he was a regular visitor to the Éclat, named Roper, and was back to report. But there was no sign at all of Bob Kerr. Nor was there a message of any kind.

For a moment or two, Tim stood nonplussed. Then an unpleasant suspicion seeped into his mind.

'I don't believe it!' he muttered, staring out into the darkness beyond the hotel entrance. 'I *can't* believe it!' But the trouble was that he could, and did.

Mr. Marcus Benson, as most of his acquaintances and all of Department Z would have acknowledged, was in many ways a remarkable man. For instance, he had appeared in several places complete with his moustache, and without making any attempt to disguise his appearance—despite the fact that he must have known that every policeman, on or off duty, and every member of the fighting services, had been furnished with a description of him and were liable to tackle him on sight. In fact, in the three weeks from the moment Toby Arran had been shot until the finding of Philip Fenway's body, seven hundred and twenty three men had been detained and inspected by Kerr, Davidson, or someone who had actually seen Benson in the flesh. None of the men had been really like Benson, but without a photograph it was impossible for the authorities to be sure that their detentions were even reasonable.

Gregory Marlin, lately one of the most successful brokers on the stock exchange, was also remarkable, although he was the first to admit that he would have been mad to have quarrelled with Benson when the first signs of trouble had developed. Benson was the active partner; Marlin made the arrangements and had no fear that they would not be carried out. But Benson was also ready to admit that without Marlin to tell him just when to act and what to do he would have been flummoxed.

Marlin had a genius for pinpointing the one thing essential to the result that he—and more particularly those who were paying him—wanted. It was Marlin who had thought of the bombing of Chicago: Marlin, who had calculated the calamitous effect of the murder of the American Ambassador.

Now Marlin and Benson sat in one of the upper rooms of the house at Putney. They never lingered downstairs, for there was just the possibility that someone might glance through a window and recognise them. It was partly this talent for eliminating every likely mischance that had given them their success so far.

Marlin's face was a little fuller than usual: he lacked exercise, and the suspense of waiting for news of his various plans gave him a thirst. Benson looked his usual self. So did the man who lounged back on a settee and listened to them both: the man who, for whatever reason, they called by the name of Mayhew.

'I think we can say,' Benson was summing up, 'that we have done very well, Marlin. Now—you said you wanted three weeks. You've had it. When can we clear out?'

Marlin rubbed his yellow skin and frowned a little.

'Not for a few days,' he said. 'There's just a little more to do, Benson. Just a little more.'

'I can't keep this thing going for ever,' Benson objected.

'No. I appreciate that. But you must remember, there is always the chance that Lilian will talk. I really didn't think she would hold out as long as she has done. And if—I say if—she does tell Craigie and that fellow Kerr all she knows, we shall still have work to do.'

'That's all very well,' Benson grumbled. 'But you can take too many chances, Marlin. We've been close enough to trouble several times.'

'But you, my excellent Benson—' Marling knew that it was almost impossible to flatter him too much—'have managed to avoid it, and I think you will have to continue to manage it.'

Benson's smile was unforced as he smoothed his hair.

'I haven't done so badly,' he agreed, with evident self-approval.

Marlin hid his own smile, and the eyes of the third man creased at the corners.

'I don't think you need worry about Lilian,' he offered. 'I've been looking after her very well.'

'Just what do you mean by "looking after"?' demanded Marlin.

'She always was very excitable,' Mayhew said, 'and she had this war bug in her bonnet. A little dosing, and she was ready to fall over the wall at any moment; you get what I mean?'

Benson frowned, unable to gather Mayhew's meaning. Marlin gathered it, all right: Mayhew had secretly accustomed Mrs. Trentham to the use of drugs, and now that she was without them, her mind was liable to crack.

'It was a great pity,' Marlin commented, 'that she ever fell into their hands.'

'It couldn't be helped,' Benson said shortly. 'I warned you right from the first that you'd be up against it with these men of Craigie's—and I might tell you, I don't like Kerr. He was close to me at Pockham, he was almighty dangerous at Preston, and Garnett tells me he was at Crayshaw last night, with Miller and one of the Arrans. He's been late, so far—but if we keep going, he'll catch up.'

Marlin's expression was inscrutable.

'You really think so?'

'Yes, I do. Supposing...' Benson leaned forward a little and Marlin could not repress a shudder as those cold, fishy eyes stared into his. 'Supposing he found *this* place. What a mess it would be!'

'He won't find it!'

'How'd he find Crayshaw?' demanded Benson.

'He has to be lucky sometimes,' Marlin retorted. 'There's

only one way he might trace us here, Benson, and that is if you're seen and followed.'

'There isn't a man on two legs,' said Benson, complacently, 'who could follow me if I didn't want him to. Don't you worry about that. *You've* caused the damage, if anyone has.'

Marlin's voice was harsher than usual.

'How?'

'The night you got away from Hendon.' Benson spread his thick hands on the desk in front of him. 'You had the other car abandoned on Wimbledon Common. If I'd been with you, it wouldn't have happened. It was too close to us.'

'The last place they'd be likely to search for us would be near where the car was abandoned,' Marlin said, irritably. 'And anyhow, that was nearly three weeks ago. Don't raise unnecessary scares, man!'

Benson shrugged.

'Well, I reckoned we'd be out of it by now: but if there's something else, what is it?'

'I haven't decided.' Marlin's very white teeth gleamed. 'I'll let you know by to-night. You'd better have your men ready.'

'They're always ready,' retorted Jacob Benson, and rose to go. 'So long, you two.'

They watched from a window as he climbed into a saloon car and disappeared down the drive and out on to the main road. Mayhew chuckled.

'He's a queer customer. As much humour as a whale, but he does do his job.'

Marlin nodded and smiled, well satisfied. If he inspired everything that happened, Benson perfected the arrangements. It had been Benson who had insisted on leaving no possible evidence at any of the places where they had been. The only records of the activities of the trio were in a safe at the Putney house—and unless the safe was opened by a key, no one would ever get at the records. Any attempt to force the lock would ignite a mechanical contrivance that would destroy all papers before the safe was open. That again was Benson's idea.

Marlin turned from the window as Mayhew offered him a cigar.

'Well... We certainly can't complain. Have you seen the papers this morning?'

'Yes.' Mayhew chuckled. He was, surprisingly, a man who found a great deal to laugh at in life. 'The scare's going well, old man. But Benson's right, you know. You can drive it too far.'

Marlin nodded.

'Yes. But I can't get away until I've collected the money, Mayhew. Our backers are notorious for their willingness to forget a debt. They want the job done properly.'

'They want,' said Mayhew, frowning, 'an actual declaration of war. It's asking a lot.'

'It's not asking the impossible. I'm surprised the declaration has been delayed so long.'

'Someone in the Government's got some sense.' Mayhew grinned. 'That's a contingency we hadn't allowed for.'

'For God's sake, don't be funny!' snapped Marlin. 'Anyhow, they didn't stipulate the declaration. All they want is a withdrawal of troops and ships from certain places. And although we haven't traced it definitely, I think the Mediterranean Fleet will shift around soon. And, of course, the Japanese are mobilising.'

Mayhew nodded, frowning.

'Yes. I've been a Lancashire man all my life—and the one country I don't like is Japan. It's ruined the mills, and I don't like to think those little yellow swine will profit.'

'They'll have their hands full,' Marlin assured him. They've trouble enough in Manchuria as it is, and they've got their eyes on Russia. They won't be anxious to start anything with America.'

'They'll follow England's lead if the thing comes,' said Mayhew. 'Take my word for it. It would be too good a chance to lose.' He rose suddenly, snapping his fingers in annoyance. 'I'm late—I must be in London by one! Before I go, Martin—do you think another week will cover us?'

'I do.' Gregory Martin smiled unpleasantly.

'And you've made all arrangements for getting out of the country?'

'Everything's ready.'

'Good,' said the man who called himself Mayhew. 'I'll see you some time tomorrow, then.'

Martin saw him to the door, then returned to his desk. He had a great many things to think about, including the final operation: the match that would ignite the ready tinder of international emotions.

14

BROKEN APPOINTMENTS

The Rt. Hon. David Wishart walked sadly from 10
Downing Street to the House of Commons. He looked
drawn and ill: even the more hostile members of the crowd
that followed him—at a reasonable distance, thanks to his
strong bodyguard—acknowledged it. Most of them also
admitted that the Prime Minister was no coward, even if he
represented a Government that was rapidly becoming unpop-
ular. He didn't try to hide himself, like some of the others: he
stuck to his habit of walking to the House every morning. He
had no intention of even appearing to submit to the prevailing
feeling of panic. In Wishart's opinion—delivered when Craigie
tried to remonstrate—it was essential for the leaders of the
country to set an example, and he proposed to do so...

It was on this particular morning that Marlin, Benson and
Mayhew had talked together at the Putney house, less than ten
miles away. The morning Press had generally been clamorous
in their demands for action. Organs that had hitherto
supported the Nationalist Cabinet through right and wrong
now turned against it. Britain, they claimed, was losing all her

pride: she was allowing America to openly accuse her of causing outrages and conniving war, and sitting down under the insult...

'It is obvious' (said the *Clarion*) *'that neither this country's Government nor that of America wishes to take the first step. That is understandable. But England must record its disapproval of the American outcry against this country. It is useless to blink at facts, and the one important fact is that America is now hostile to Great Britain. Already, there is a concentration of troops on the Canadian border. Unless immediate steps are taken, America will throw its forces against Canada, and take that vast stretch of country—rich in natural wealth, one of our greatest and fairest dominions—from under our very noses. This danger is imminent. What is the Government going to do?'*

In the House that morning Wishart was faced with similar criticism from Opposition benches. He knew, also, that a great proportion of National Members were opposed to his policy of inaction. The Whips had kept the Government from falling, but a safe majority of three hundred had been turned into a narrow one of seventy-odd on three occasions, and there was no telling when the back-benchers might not rise *en masse* against the Cabinet.

Perhaps it was Wishart's personality that kept the vote with him. He stood out, those days, as a man who could be obstinate, could be blind, but who certainly stood by his convictions in a way that commanded respect. He listened to the criticism white-faced, his hands clenched. When a storm of cheers broke out after the Leader of the Opposition's particularly biting speech, Wishart stood up abruptly.

There was something in his manner that demanded silence, and he spoke to a quieter House than he had addressed for weeks. His opening words sent a rustle through the benches. He ignored the formal opening, and his voice was quivering.

'Gentlemen,' he began, 'are we all fools? Do we *want* war, to see our people massacred, our homes smashed down? Do we want an international holocaust? Are we going to let pride and pomposity dictate to us? Or are we sane men, trying to effect conciliation by discussion, settlement of disputes by arbitration? Are we in the Dark Ages, or is this the twentieth century? Do you want your Government to show a lack of restraint that will bring this country to war with America, or are you prepared to let the voice of reason speak for you, to wait until this anti-American wave of public feeling has settled down, until Americans, at heart our friends, have recovered from their wave of hysteria? Gentlemen—it is in your hands...

Wishart spoke for five minutes—and his impassioned appeal, followed by a snap Division, won a vote of confidence by a majority of seventy-eight. It was a triumph, but it merely delayed what many considered the inevitable.

Craigie and Kerr admired his efforts and realised their full worth.

Wishart, they had learned, had suffered badly from Marlin's activities. He was not a wealthy man, and had lost as much, if not more, than Sir Kenneth Halloway when Marlin had cashed in before his disappearance. These financial worries naturally added to the Premier's burden. At the other end of the line, Halloway was rich; he even went so far as to offer private money for the defence of England, although the offer was refused with due ceremony. He had lost his twenty thousand pounds worth of bonds to Marlin, but if proof were needed of his financial stability, it was soon forthcoming.

In his own way, Halloway was devoting all he possessed to the country.

Before accepting the post of Under-Secretary to the Ministry of Defence, he had relinquished his seat on the Boards of three armament companies, and the Potter Mills, and had put all his shares on the market.

The sale of all those shares had been negotiated through Marlin, which accounted for Halloway's somewhat bitter remarks anent that gentleman. Those remarks, however, were nothing to Sir James Cathie's, although Cathie had little or no cause for complaint. He had extensive shares in many Government-contract companies: and although he had not advertised the fact, had of late bought substantially in Dickers-Leestrong, perhaps the largest armament manufacturers in the country, and was making money hand over fist. Perhaps it was the knowledge that he could have bought Wishart out a hundred times that made him sniff disparagingly at the Premier's speech: certainly he made it clear he thought the danger was absurdly exaggerated.

Timothy Arran reached the Carilon Club after a visit to Toby, who was by now being kept in the hospital under protest. Kerr and Wally Davidson were there and he waved a newspaper at them, as he cheerfully announced:

'Prime Minister makes impassioned appeal, and the loyal British public pats his back. Another reprieve, you fellows, and now we've *got* to get to work.'

Kerr's smile had little humour in it.

'How?' he demanded. 'We're stuck. Up against the proverbial brick wall. We've searched Marlin's place, Potter's place, Crayshaw and a dozen other spots, and we haven't found a single thing. We haven't even found the motive.'

Timothy nodded, subdued now.

'It's a brute, old boy. I know: 'I've never struck anything like it. I can't see the slightest glimmer of sense in the whole thing. Who the hell *wants* us to fight America, anyhow?'

Davidson shrugged his shoulders, and Kerr grimaced.

'There are reasons,' he said, 'but they're best not talked about.'

'I suppose not.' Timothy shrugged. Then remembered: 'Oh, and that reminds me, *Mister* Kerr. What the blazes do you mean by dodging off last night, after pushing me on to the man with a limp? He's as innocent of intrigue as a new-born babe!'

'He might not have been,' Kerr hedged.

'You know damned well you pushed me on to him so you could slide out after Penelope and her uncle!'

'Did I?' murmured Robert McMillan Kerr. 'I don't remember.'

He would not be drawn further. He had followed Penelope because he wanted to assure himself that she and her uncle did visit the London home of the Potter Company's solicitor. They had done so, and indeed had stayed until half-past eleven, before returning to the Éclat Hotel, from which Mark Potter had gone to his fiat. Kerr was still not satisfied about Penelope, but he could not bring himself to believe she was knowingly concerned in the campaign of madness that threatened to lead the way to world disaster.

'Oh well,' Timothy said, 'if you won't talk, you won't. But harm a hair of that lass's head, and I wouldn't be in your shoes.'

'I was worried before,' murmured Kerr drily, 'and I'm terrified, now. Tim, I want you and Wally to go to Dorchester. There's a gas factory there, and a spot of trouble with our Communist friends. Halloway's reported it. It *might* be a blind, but Benson could be behind it. The O.C. is a man named Carter. I know him slightly and you'll find him a good fellow.'

'Right,' said Timothy. 'We're on our way.'

Kerr stayed on for ten minutes or so, alone, and listened to a dozen conversations between members both young and, old. The same talk was here as was in the streets. Grey-beards and downy-chins wagged to the same refrain. It was bound to come soon. Inevitable. And the sooner—said some—the better.

Kerr swung out of the room savagely. The blind fools couldn't see what would happen if it did come!

He was stopped at the main door by an attendant.

'Excuse me, sir, but do you know if Mr. Arran's gone?'

'Yes,' said Kerr, 'ten minutes ago.' And added, since any message for Timothy might well be connected with the job in hand: 'Can I help?'

'Well sir—there's a lady on the telephone says she wants to get in touch with him urgently. You don't know where he's gone, sir?'

'I've several ideas,' Kerr told him. 'I'll speak with her.'

He went to the telephone, seeing in his mind's eye as he spoke to her, the fair face of Penelope Smith. Her pleasant voice strengthened the vision.

'That's not you, Timothy?'

'Afraid not. But can I help, Miss Smith? Kerr here.'

There was a moment's pause before she answered, dubiously.

'I don't know... You'll probably think me a fool, Mr. Kerr.'

'Chance it,' Kerr invited, and she did.

'It's about my uncle, Mr.—oh *damn*! I'm not going to call you "Mister". Listen Bob. He's missing.'

'Who?' Kerr demanded. 'Mark Potter?'

'Yes. I'd arranged to meet him here at eleven o'clock, for

more of this business with the solicitors, and he hasn't arrived. I know it's only twelve, but he's the most punctual man I know, and—well, after the affair at Preston, I'm worried.'

'Yes—naturally. You've telephoned his flat?'

'He left there at ten-forty. That would have given him just time to get to the Éclat by eleven.'

'Yes,' Kerr decided. 'It's worth looking into, Penelope. Can you meet me at his flat in, say, half-an-hour?'

'At his flat?'

'Yes.'

'All right,' she said, 'I'll be there.'

Kerr rang off, then dialled Craigie's number. A few minutes talk with the Chief of Z was enough, and within another five, he had collected his car from the Mall, and was on his way to Mark Potter's flat in St. John's Wood at a speed that shocked all who saw him—except the police, who knew the number of his big Benz tourer and had instructions not to stop it on any account.

Kerr reached the flat fifteen minutes before Penelope was due, and spent them in trying to discover whether Potter had given any indication that he might not be going to keep his appointment with the girl, and whether he had had any unidentifiable visitors or telephone calls.

According to Potter's man—whose name, by some quirk of coincidence was Clay—nothing at all had happened out of the ordinary. Mark Potter's life was a well-ordered one, and Clay had served him for fifteen years without knowing it any different. Of course, he did not keep regular hours, but he always told Clay when to expect his return.

At twelve-thirty Penelope had not appeared; at twelve-forty Superintendent Miller, big and capable-looking as ever, arrived with two plainclothes men, for Kerr did not propose to take chances again. There was just the possibility that Mark

Potter *did* know something about this business, and that there would be records to say so in the flat or in the London office of the Potter Mills.

At one-twenty, Miller reported there was nothing at all to suggest that anything was amiss. But Penelope Smith had not arrived.

Penelope Smith had left the Éclat Hotel at twelve-five. She felt like walking, and knew that if she found herself late, she could take a taxi when she was nearer the flat. She had been walking for ten minutes and was near Marble Arch when she saw her uncle.

Mark Potter was sitting in the rear of a Daimler saloon. He was not alone, and she only glimpsed him for a moment before the car was past. But she was already on edge: she didn't believe he would have missed their meeting deliberately, without letting her know, and on the spur of the moment she beckoned a taxi. As it pulled up, she asked quickly:

'Do you think you can keep that Daimler in sight?'

'I'll try, lady,' said the cabby, and Penelope stepped in. She realised ruefully that Bob Kerr would feel he had more reason than ever for disliking her, but she was far more concerned with the possibility that Mark Potter was somehow mixed up in a business which had already proved fatal to his brother.

The Daimler stopped outside the Chelsea Town Hall, and its driver went into a small tobacconist's shop nearby. Penelope told her cabby to drive past, but to get at a corner where he could turn either way in a hurry. For twenty minutes the man was busy in the shop. The thing seemed queerer than ever, and she watched impatiently. If she got out and telephoned Kerr, she might lose the Daimler, and she had no desire to do that. It was twenty minutes later—at five to one—when the driver returned to the big saloon and started off again. This time, it moved towards Fulham—and very soon it was travelling over Putney Bridge.

The Daimler obligingly did not make much speed, even in unrestricted areas. At the top of Putney Hill it turned right, and at Roehampton village it stopped at a garage; again the driver got out and again kept the occupants of the car waiting for several minutes. Penelope knew what Mark Potter would have said about that, in normal circumstances—and liked the look of this whole business less and less.

'I'm being a fool,' she scolded herself, 'but what else can I do? Oh thank goodness, it's started again!'

Again, the Daimler moved off, and the cab followed. Penelope knew that part of London well, and frowned when she saw that it was taking a different road, but heading back towards Putney. Trying to make sense of it all, she sat back and closed her eyes.

When she opened them, she knew that what was about to happen was inevitable.

A large, black car was coming towards them. It had passed the Daimler in which her uncle was riding, and was within twenty yards of the taxi when Penelope looked up, and she was in time to see it swerve towards them and its driver jump out. She opened her mouth in a silent scream and shrank back against the cushions for what seemed like an age.

Then the crash came. She felt the terrific impact, felt something smash against her head: and then, oblivion...

15
FEARS FOR PENELOPE

The call went out for Penelope Smith at one thirty-five, for Kerr was now very anxious indeed to find her. The reply came more quickly than he had expected, and certainly in a very different form. He was at Scotland Yard with Miller when the telephone rang, and Miller took the instrument.

'Yes—I *do*. What's that?'

Kerr needed no telling that this concerned Penelope Smith; a single glance at Miller's face was enough, as he grunted a final: 'I'll go there,' and hung up.

'She's been in a smash,' he said simply. 'At Wimbledon. She's in hospital there, now. Concussion—and still unconscious. Driver of her cab dead.'

Bob Kerr drew a deep breath, his expression grim.

'An accident, eh? I wonder. And I wonder what she was doing at Wimbledon?'

'She might be able to talk when we get there,' said Miller. 'If you want to come?'

'I certainly do,' Kerr jumped up. 'And the quicker the better. But wait a minute...' He was frowning as he tried to fathom why he had felt instinctively that he had missed some vital clue. Then remembered: 'Wimbledon! I knew it had been mentioned the car Marlin escaped in was found there, wasn't it?'

'It was indeed!' said Miller.

Kerr gave a lop-sided grin. 'We're jumping to some pretty broad conclusions,' he warned. 'But will you send out a call for the Wimbledon area to be specially watched? I'll get Craigie on another line.'

It was typical of the situation that Craigie agreed with Kerr that immediate action was necessary. In many cases, the facts would have been considered no more than coincidence; now they were looked on as likely evidence.

'Who've you got in London?' Kerr asked.

'Carruthers,' said Craigie. 'He's at his flat at Putney. Came back from the north last night. I'll telephone him to meet you at the Bridge.'

'And you can pick Trale up at his flat. And Beaumont. That enough?'

'It should be,' Kerr thanked him 'with some of Miller's men.'

Miller used a police Talbot, taking three plainclothes men with him. Kerr, in the Benz, called for Beaumont—a languid soul with some affinity to Wally Davidson; but like Wally, very useful in a scrap and always ready for trouble.

Trale was awakened from what he claimed was his first sleep for weeks, but when he heard of the accident to Penelope Smith he forgot his tiredness and urged Kerr to hurry. Bob Carruthers was waiting on the far side of the bridge in his Singer two-seater, and the three cars sped up Putney Hill towards Wimbledon, passed the house called Common View, without seeing Benson, Marlin or Mayhew—who was also present—or Mark Potter. And without being seen, which was probably more important.

They reached the hospital to find Penelope in reasonably good shape. A gash across her forehead was heavily bandaged, but she had escaped lightly. The Lanchester which had smashed into the taxi had torn the front to bits, but would have done considerably more damage had the driver not slowed down to jump, thus lessening the impact.

'Can you tell us anything, Penelope?' Kerr asked.

'A bit.' She felt too ill even to try to smile. She already knew of the taxi-driver's death and felt herself to blame for it. 'I saw Uncle Mark in a car—a Daimler—and I followed it. It stopped once or twice—'

'Can you tell me where?'

'Yes...' She sighed and closed her eyes, and the nurse who was watching frowned and wondered why this interrogation had been allowed: it could set her patient back a week or more. 'A small tobacconist's next to Chelsea Town Hall. And—a garage in Roehampton.'

'Good girl,' Kerr approved. He was torn between a burning anxiety to get all possible information, and a wish that he need not harass her. He made a mental note to get one of Miller's men to telephone a message to Tim's manservant as quickly as possible, as he asked easily: 'Anything else?'

'No. I just saw—the car—'

She shuddered. Bob Kerr, surprisingly, put a hand over hers and pressed it gently.

'It's all right,' he soothed. 'And thank you, Penelope. You've been a brick.'

Miller arranged for telephone messages to the Chelsea police and also to the Arran flat, while Kerr, Carruthers and Trale started for Roehampton. A somewhat envious Beaumont waited at the hospital in case Penelope said anything that should be relayed to Craigie.

There were two garages at the Roehampton side of the Common. Kerr tackled one; Trale and Carruthers the other. It was Kerr who had the luck.

A grimy lad in a once-white suit of overalls was surprised and annoyed by Kerr's brusque:

'I don't want any petrol, thanks. Have you had a Daimler here this afternoon?'

'Supposing I have?'

Kerr inwardly cursed himself, outwardly smiled, and showed a ten shilling note.

'Have you?' he asked again.

The lad's eyes brightened.

'Well, sir, now you come to mention it, we did 'ave a Daimler. Took six gallons: Driver used the phone, too—and mighty fussy no one could hear what he said.'

'Was he, then!' After three weeks without clue of any kind, Kerr perhaps felt more cheered than the statement warranted. 'You didn't recognise him, I suppose?'

'Well, he looked kind of familiar.' The lad was in possession of the note now, and prepared to call on imagination as well as memory. But the arrival of the garage proprietor saved the day. 'Gent here been asking about that Daimler, Bert,' the lad explained, as Kerr nodded pleasantly to the newcomer. 'The one as used the phone, remember?'

Bert did, and Kerr could hardly believe his luck. For the driver had been so anxious to have the office to himself, while making his call, that the proprietor had thought it just possible the till was the real object, and had gone outside to make a note of the Daimler's number. And there it was, where he'd scribbled it on the back of an old envelope: EXL 8013.

'A black saloon, it was, sir: 1936 model. I've seen it about this way several times.'

'Thanks—you've helped a lot,' Kerr told him, with real feeling, and Bert grinned as he took the famous flyer's hand.

'Proud to know I have, Mr. Kerr,' he said. 'Knew you the moment I saw you!'

The young attendant stared after the Benz a moment later, his face twisted in awe.

'Blimey!' he said. 'Reckon he thinks he's flying the ruddy thing. Ever see anything move like that?'

'I'll see you move like it, if you don't run a rag over those pumps,' his boss informed him. 'Get a move on, and mind your own business.'

And neither of them ever knew just how vital a part they had played in the affair that was even at that moment making the whole world tremble.

The three Department Z men had arranged to meet Miller again at the Wimbledon police station, and Carruthers and Trale came in as Miller was telling Kerr that EXL 8013 was a Lancashire number. Which meant that the Daimler—if genuinely registered under that number and not fitted with a false number plate—must have started its career in the north. While Miller telephoned the Yard to start a nation-wide search for it, Kerr talked with the station sergeant.

A half-hour passed—with Kerr conscious at every moment how often he had previously traced Benson just too late to prevent some further outrage—before they were able to meet and question two beat policemen, who had seen a car with that number-plate in the area quite often. But when they did, both men agreed that it came from one of the larger houses lining the Common.

Kerr waited with what patience he could find as the pair rapidly changed out of uniform. Then with Miller beside him, and Carruthers and Trale following on, he drove off with them along the Wimbledon-Putney road. And as they passed the gates of Common View, the younger constable broke the silence.

That's the place, sir, I'm sure!'

Miller grunted, and addressed the other man:

'Recognise it, Ramage?'

'I think it's the place, sir.' Ramage was cautious: he was an older man, and knew what harm misplaced confidence could do. He turned to peer back at the tree-lined drive. 'Yes... Yes, I'm sure that's the one, sir.'

'Good,' said Miller. 'What do you want to do, Kerr?'

'Well, you're top priority, right now, so I'll get you back to the station, pronto. But Carruthers and Trale can keep watch from the Common, meantime—we'll stop them a bit further along. Then while you're organising things your side, I'll dig out what I can on this "Common View". Can one of you tell me,' he added over his shoulder, 'Where I'll find the Town Hall —and whether they keep the Rating department there?'

'They do, sir,' said Ramage. 'And we can both lead you there blindfold.'

'Good,' said Kerr.

He stopped a couple of hundred yards up the road, and Trale and Carruthers pulled up behind. They were well pleased at the prospect of action and went off eagerly to begin their vigil. Kerr drove Miller to the Wimbledon police station and left him arranging for a strong cordon of men to be thrown around the house, while he himself made his enquiries at the Town Hall. His temporary police agent's card assured him immediate attention, and he learned that the registered owner of the house was a Mr. Peterson, but that a Colonel

Piper lived there. Piper, it seemed, was well known in the neighbourhood and if considered by some to be a little starchy and military, was liked well enough. The rates of the house were paid promptly, and nothing in the nature of suspicion had fallen on the man.

'As a matter of fact, sir,' said the Rating Officer who gave him this information, 'Mr. Reynoldson—the Town Clerk—lives next door to the Colonel. He might be able to give you more information.'

Kerr thanked him with a dazzling smile. He could still hardly credit that the luck was at last breaking his way. 'Where is his office?'

'The next door along, sir, on the right. But...'

'I'll be back in five minutes,' said Robert Kerr.

At the door marked 'Town Clerk—Private,' he tapped and walked in. The man sitting at the large desk facing him looked up in surprise.

'Who are you, sir?' he demanded sharply.

'My name's Kerr,' said Kerr, 'from Scotland Yard. I'm sorry to intrude, Mr. Reynoldson, but you can give me valuable information on a matter that is vital and urgent. It concerns a Colonel Piper...'

Whether this direct approach took the Town Clerk's fancy, whether he was perturbed by mention of Scotland Yard, or whether Piper's name surprised him Kerr could not guess. But the Town Clerk gestured to a chair and he echoed the name.

'Colonel Piper?'

'Yes,' said Kerr. 'Will you listen a moment?'

He said enough to make Reynoldson's face pale, and followed with a quiet:

'Can you give me any information at all about the man?'

Reynoldson pursed his lips.

'No information that would interest you, Mr. Kerr, but one

or two curious things. For instance, although Piper is a man of independent means and certainly does not attend any business, he has a great number of callers who always come and go by car. I've learned this,' the Town Clerk apologised with a smile, 'from the tittle-tattle of my butler. The only other thing is that Piper seems to have—almost an obsession, about burglars. He takes extreme precautions, certainly.'

'He does, does he?' murmured Kerr, and rose to go. 'I don't think I need worry you any more at the moment, Mr. Reynoldson. Many thanks, indeed!'

Ramage was waiting in the Benz outside, and five minutes saw them at the Station again. Miller was on the steps, waiting. He hopped into the car as Ramage jumped out, and Kerr hardly stopped it. As they went, he reported what he had discovered, and learned in turn that a force of thirty armed policemen were concentrating on Common View.

'What are you going to do?' Miller asked.

'Load Carruthers and Trale into this,' said Kerr without hesitation, 'and introduce myself to Colonel Piper. I'm sure he'll be surprised to see me. And I wonder if we'll find any of our other birds?'

'If you do, there'll be trouble,' Miller warned grimly.

'I know.' Bob Kerr was smiling with something very like contentment. 'This will be warm, all right, but—with a little luck, Miller, *we've got them!*'

Craigie, or any man who had worked for or with Department Z in the past ten years, could have told Kerr that never in the Department's history had there been an affair like that of Marlin and Benson. There were three vital differences, and several subsidiary ones that had a bearing on the issue.

First, there was the absolute lack of clues, and the complete disappearance of all the men connected with the case directly the Department began to realise they were suspect. Second, there were the long—two or three days was a long time, in the work of Department Z, where a day's delay might mean life or death for hundreds—periods of futile working, of following wasted trail after wasted trail.

Third, there had been that peculiar method of attack by Benson; his was a type of ruthlessness that even Craigie had rarely encountered.

In some ways, Kerr's attitude was similar to Benson's. Craigie, who saw a great deal more of this business than many would have believed, knew that although Kerr had uncovered very little, although the case was dragging out dangerously, although the issues were bigger, probably than any that had gone before, his new agent was the most disconcertingly direct man he had ever used. He acted the moment there was so much as a whisper to suggest a move in any direction; and he moved incredibly fast.

At two forty-five that afternoon neither Kerr nor Benson dreamed they were within a hundred yards of each other. This was when Kerr at the wheel of his Benz, and Carruthers and Trale in the rear, began to turn into the drive of Common View.

Benson was with Marlin in the first-floor study. He had called to arrange for the final preparations of the thing that was, without shadow of doubt, to spark the international blaze. Marlin had talked to certain gentlemen, who proposed to meet his asking price of one million pounds, plus expenses, and both parties were well pleased with progress. Having just accepted a large sum in cash, Benson was grinning his satisfaction as he prepared to leave.

'That's all right, then, Marlin. They'll go up tonight. Not a minute before or after, take my word.'

Marlin eyed him with mingled admiration and contempt.

'You're a cool devil,' he said, dispassionately.

'I know my job.' Benson grinned again. 'I'll be seeing you, Marlin.'

'If there's any emergency,' Marlin began: 'ring...'

Cutting across his words came the roar of a high-powered car, the skidding of wheels and the screeching of brakes. As both men moved instinctively to the window, they saw the Benz swing suicidally into the drive.

'What the devil...' muttered Marlin.

'*Kerr!*' swore Benson, and leapt for the bell-push on Marlin's desk as the big car rushed towards the house. He had pressed it before Marlin fully realised what he had meant. *Kerr*! Kerr—*Craigie's* man—*here!*

Benson was cool and collected, now; a better man in emergency than Marlin: 'That's the doors locked, all right—but they'll try the windows.'

'But what...?'

'We're going to fight!' snarled Benson, suddenly turning on the man who had given him this job. 'If they catch us, we'll hang. And if they don't, we'll be shot—or they will.'

Marlin's eyes bulged.

'But there must be another way!' he protested.

'Sure—fighting.' Benson had recovered from his outburst. 'Telephone the garage and—'

What else he would have said was drowned in the appalling din of the crash. As a cloud of dust billowed upwards, the sudden bellowing of voices from below-stairs added to the row.

'They've smashed the windows!' Benson snapped. 'There's not much you can teach Kerr. Come on, blast you—call the garage.'

16

END OF A GENTLEMAN

'I f the door won't open, try the windows,' Carruthers had advised Kerr, more in fun than earnest. But Kerr had raced the Benz along the drive, slowed down as he crashed over shrubs and flower-beds, and was travelling at five miles an hour when the radiator of the big car crashed through the spacious window of an unused drawing-room.

Kerr had judged it to a nicety, with little damage done to the car; but Carruthers and Trale swore as they ducked to avoid flying glass. Kerr didn't seem to notice it. He was out of his seat as the car reached a standstill, and scrambling rapidly over the radiator to jump into the room.

'My God,' Carruthers murmured. 'That man isn't human!'

'Nor are you,' grinned Trale. 'Come on!'

They jumped after him, but in the room with the gaping window, only an open door told them where he had gone. A split second later, they heard his voice:

'Oh, no you don't!'

Then a sound as if Kerr had used his fist and not his gun.

He had.

He had told himself, from the moment he suspected this house to be connected with Marlin and Benson—and quite probably to shelter their men—that there was just one way to go about this: to smash a way in. He guessed the occupiers would soon be warned of any massing of police—and he had no desire to give the gang-leader a second's warning. Shock tactics were the only kind likely to succeed.

He went through the first room with his automatic in his left hand and his right clenched ready for an emergency. It came in the form of a man who had raced through from the rear of the house to reach the hall as Kerr himself did. The man grabbed for his gun: Kerr didn't bother. He smashed his fist into the man's face and sent him reeling, and the crack as his head struck the wall assured him there would be no more immediate trouble from that quarter.

At the foot of the stairs, he hesitated.

There was need for caution now, for attacks might come from any direction. He waited what seemed an interminable time before Carruthers and Trale appeared. He heard them and snapped:

'Try those rooms.'

"Those rooms" were three that opened from the hall. Carruthers and Trale tried them, ready to shoot and be shot at; but all were empty.

'Trale,' Kerr ordered. 'Stay put by the stairs. The police will be here any minute.'

'I'll let 'em in,' Trale grinned. 'Promise.'

Kerr flashed a grim smile, then started up the stairs, two at a time. He knew that the occupants of the house must be aware of trouble, or more than one of them would have appeared by now.

If Benson were here...

Kerr and the gang-leader caught sight of each other at the

same moment. Kerr was at the top of the stairs as Benson cautiously opened the door of the room in which he and Marlin were sheltering. His gun and Kerr's spat at the same time, but even as the flames stabbed out, Kerr had ducked and a bullet cracked into the wall behind him, showering plaster on Carruther's head. Kerr's own pecked into the door as Benson slammed it.

'He's in there,' Kerr murmured.

'Got him!' Carruthers said, with patent satisfaction.

'I'm not so sure—*get down!*'

The shout followed the opening of a door at the far end of the landing, and made a startled Carruthers drop to the boards quicker than he had ever dropped before. Kerr followed suit just as the hail of bullets swept over them. He could see the snout of the gun and the hand of the man holding it, and touched the trigger of his automatic.

The man screeched, the gun sagged, emptying itself into the floor. Kerr snapped: 'Stay here, but find cover!' and — although lying full length—somehow levered himself up and executed a prodigious leap forward, in one smooth movement.

The far door was still partly open, held there by the machine-gun, which lay where it had fallen. He knew the sudden quiet might well be a ruse, but it didn't stop him. He pushed the door open another five inches, but the body of the man was obviously blocking it. He could get the machine-gun out now, though, and pocketed his automatic quickly as he did so.

Then he put his shoulder to the door and pushed hard. As it cleared the obstacle and swung back, he had the gun ready. But the room was empty, save for the man on the floor, who had caught the bullet in his chest. Kerr's mind was still ablaze. He wanted Benson and Marlin, and as the moments flew, he grew afraid that they might yet escape. But outside, the place was crowded with police: no-one who tried to get past the cordon could succeed. No-one—

Kerr moved as the thought struck him. He had been surprised that there were so comparatively few men here; but this was probably a headquarters: Benson would house his gunmen somewhere else. For the moment, what mattered was the room where he had seen the gang-leader.

Carruthers was sheltering behind a large cupboard from which he could survey seven or eight of the doors in the two passages leading from the landing. His gun was in his hand, but he grinned as he saw the tommy-gun in Kerr's.

'Sauce for the goose,' he murmured.

'Be ready for it,' Kerr warned, unsmiling.

He put the snout of the machine-gun two inches from the lock, and pressed the trigger. The thing trembled in his hands almost like a pneumatic drill, and bullets chipped into the wood. For perhaps a minute he kept it up, and then the door sagged inwards.

'Wait,' Kerr cautioned.

It was impossible to know what would happen, Benson may have escaped through another door, or he might be waiting—and with his gun.

'Carruthers—see if you can find me a padded chair.'

He indicated the door as he spoke, and Carruthers nodded understanding and hurried off. He knew it would be madness to try any of the upper rooms, there was no knowing who might be in them. The uncertainty—the silence—was unnerving. Trale was looking fidgety at the foot of the stairs.

'No police; no nothing,' he reported.

'There will be.' Carruthers patted him on the head—much to Trale's annoyance, for Dodo was never at his best when waiting for things to happen—and went into the room with the smashed window. There was just the chair Kerr wanted and he took it up, puffing a little, for the furniture in the house was old and heavy.

Kerr was waiting, his face set:

'No sound of any kind,' he muttered.

'That's what Dodo's complaining of. *And* no police.'

'They won't come into the grounds until I send for them. They're outside to stop the rats running. I've heard,' he added morosely, as Carruthers crouched behind the chair and held it by its front legs to push it against the door, 'of tunnels and passages to nearby houses. I hope we haven't struck anything like that.'

Carruthers was still pushing slowly and both men were crouching behind the chair, Kerr with the Thomson in his hands. The door opened six inches—a foot—two feet. No sound came.

'Steady!' Kerr whispered sharply, as Carruthers grew impatient or optimistic and took three inches at the same time. 'Benson's as cunning as a fox.'

'Sorry,' mouthed Carruthers.

As he said it, Kerr took the chance of glancing quickly over the top of the chair. It was a risk, but few risks could have been more justified. For Kerr saw it coming—a little round, black thing which curled through the air, with a trail of smoke behind it.

'What the hell!' snapped Carruthers.

Because Kerr had suddenly leapt from their cover. He caught a glimpse of Marlin and Benson in one corner of the room and saw Benson's hand move, with the gun in it. He felt the pain as the bullet snicked his hand, but it didn't stop him. He stretched his right hand upwards and clutched, as he would have clutched at a slip catch going over his head. He felt the thing touch and then stop, caught by his fingertips.

Carruthers swore when he saw what it was.

Marlin screamed and Benson fired, again, but he lost his aim as he saw what was coming and made a desperate leap to one side. Kerr held the bomb for something under a split-second, then hurled it back—not at the window, but at the two men. He dropped behind the chair as it went, and saw Benson flinging himself on the floor. He just glimpsed Marlin, a few inches from the bomb and standing as though petrified, before the explosion came.

Carruthers and Kerr felt the blast suck at them, and heard the bang and the smashing of glass—and the high-pitched screech that preceded the explosion by a second or less. They felt the chair lift in the air; but they clutched at it like grim death, and it saved them as nothing else could have done.

The room seemed to be rocking, under a dense shower of dust and debris from the walls and the ceiling. Kerr didn't know what had happened to Benson, but he had a shrewd idea that Marlin had gone from this world for ever, and even in that moment he felt a fierce exultation.

'Watch the right-hand corner,' he warned abruptly.

Cautiously, he rose to survey the scene. The chaos in front of him was indescribable. So were the blotches of red on the walls, and other, grimmer things. Benson was still on the floor, lying very still.

Kerr didn't need the machine-gun now. He stepped past the chair, automatic in hand...

He saw Benson move suddenly, and tightened his grip on the gun, prepared for anything. He hardly saw the thing that Benson flicked towards him and Carruthers. Not until it struck against the wall with a little tinkling sound did he realise what it might be; and by then the, sickly smell was in his nostrils and he felt his senses reeling. He fired twice, but didn't know whether he'd found his man as he staggered back-wards, taking Carruthers with him.

One thing and one thing only saved their lives.

The gas wouldn't kill them, but Benson would have shot them if he could. It would have taken time, and he dared not risk even an extra second. He had drawn a deep breath as he flung the phial of gas and dared not take another until he was out of range. Moreover, he could already hear footsteps on the stairs.

He reached the head of them before taking in that second breath, and by that time, Dodo Trale was half-way up. Benson was prepared for action, and he fired first. And as Dodo felt the bullet bite into his shin and went down, Benson leapt over him.

There were shadows on the front door now, and men were thundering on it; but he knew that the doors were locked and that dynamite alone would force them. The windows were the answer.

Benson wasn't thinking of anything then, but the job of getting away. He didn't waste time on regrets or curses. He was the nearest imaginable thing to a fighting machine: he was prepared to get through alive or die fighting.

He swung round at the foot of the stairs towards the servant's quarters and the garage behind the house. The car would be waiting there—if the police hadn't reached it first. But luck was with him, and he climbed through the kitchen window to see the car standing ready, out of the garage. The men were gone; his instructions had been that they should prepare the car and then save themselves. True, they were probably in the hands of the attackers, but they didn't know much, and Benson couldn't afford to worry about others as well as himself.

He was grinning mirthlessly as he reached the car. He did not carry a gun, but in his left hand were three of the small glass phials.

He put them gently in the dash-board pocket—a pocket specially lined for them—and pressed the self-starter. He could see the police now, approaching from the properties on either side and along the main drive. But he had a trick or two ready for them. He turned the nose of the car towards a wall that looked to be of solid brick, a spot which the police had ignored; he revved from ten to thirty miles an hour in the forty feet he had to spare, and smashed through the wall as though through paper—which is what that section consisted of. And now, he was on the drive of the next house—the house of Mr. Reynoldson, the Town Clerk.

The police were mostly behind him, appalled and bewildered. They fired after him, but the bullets whanged uselessly against armoured wings and panels as Benson trod on the accelerator. When he reached the exit gate of the drive, he was touching fifty.

The three men standing there waited to the last moment, to be surer of their aim—and their caution cost them their victim. For as the car drew level with them, Benson tossed one of his little phials—and his worries from that quarter were over.

He went out of the drive on three wheels, tyres screeching and engine roaring. A dozen police, bunched together, were waiting with their guns. Stabs of flame darted towards the car, but the tyres escaped. Two bullets struck Benson, but did little damage; far less, certainly, than the havoc caused as he flung another gas-bomb. And then he was on the main road, and could let the car all out. If nothing got in his way, he could make it. If something got in his way, it couldn't be helped. In any case, Wimbledon Common gave him a fighting chance.

17
KERR'S BRIGHT NOTIONS

K err came round with a head ready to burst, and suffered five minutes of retching that seemed to turn him inside out. By the time he had recovered from it he felt weak and fit for nothing but a long night's sleep. His face was very pale, but his eyes were hard. He looked up at the faces of two or three strange men—and one solid, familiar figure.

'How do you feel?' asked Superintendent Miller.

'Swinish,' said Kerr, 'Give me a hand up, will you?'

Miller glanced at a sober-looking man beside him, who nodded agreement.

'He'll be all right.'

'Thanks, doctor,' said Miller, and helped Kerr up.

He staggered as he reached his feet, and would have fallen but for Miller's steadying arm. After a moment, he hobbled to a chair and sat down. They were in the front room of the house into which he had burst something under forty minutes earlier.

'Well?' he queried, drily.

'Benson managed it,' Miller said, with a gloomy smile. 'He

189

had one too many tricks in his bag. We've caught a couple of his men, though—and the chap who calls himself Colonel Piper.' He grimaced sourly. 'This thing apart, he'd be for the long drop.'

'Like that, eh?' said Kerr. 'I wonder what Reynoldson will think of that.' He closed his eyes for a moment, trying to pull himself together, and when he opened them again he seemed more alert.

'Find me a spot of whisky, someone will you? What's doing Miller?'

'We're turning the place inside out,' Miller told him, as one of the local men went for the whisky. 'But nothing's been reported so far. I daresay one of the prisoners will talk, though.'

'If they know anything, that's fine,' said Kerr.

He took the whisky, and felt a new man a couple of minutes later. Even his legs would bear him without tottering, although he was still a little shaky. For the first time he saw Carruthers, still unconscious, and cocked an enquiring eyebrow at the medico.

'He'll pull round, all right,' said that worthy. 'He got more of it than you. But it's not lethal.'

'Good. How about Trale?'

'Shot in the leg,' said Miller, with a ghost of a smile. 'You can almost hear what he thinks about it if you listen. He's on a couch in the other room. Nothing serious.'

'So the damage might have been worse?' Kerr suggested.

'From our side, a lot worse. We've done more to-day than in the last month. Three prisoners and a man dead upstairs. Or what,' Miller corrected, with grisly precision, 'there is left of him. What happened?'

'He threw a bomb and I threw it back,' said Kerr, offhandedly. 'Does Craigie know about this?'

'He's on his way.'

'Good! I think I'll take it easy until he comes.'

The remark brought a smile from the doctor, who would have recommended that Kerr took it easily for the next ten days at least. Perhaps because they had been in the confines of the house, Kerr and Carruthers had suffered more from the gas than anyone else; Kerr had been out for twenty minutes and his friend was only now recovering. A round dozen of the police had been out for periods of five to fifteen minutes.

Kerr sat back in an easy chair, while Miller and his men searched the house and everything in it.

The Department Z man was resting physically, but not mentally. He regretted the fact that Benson had managed to get away, but he was thanking the fates that he and his men had suffered so lightly. It might have been a great deal worse; in fact, it was a miracle it had not been.

Several things puzzled him, especially after he heard how Benson had crashed through the dummy wall. Why had Benson and Marlin not made for the garage immediately, and tried to get away? Of course, from the moment when they had crashed into the window to the moment he had reached the head of the stairs, something under two minutes had passed. Benson hadn't had much time.

If Kerr hadn't glanced up as the bomb had come, he and Carruthers would have been in perdition now, and both the crooks would have escaped. He guessed that only lack of time had stopped Benson from shooting him after the gassing. And he had tossed that bomb in the hope of destroying both Department men: Benson's attitude to those who worked for Craigie was written very plain: 'kill or be killed'.

But what now? If Marlin had been the prime mover in this thing, there was a good chance of stopping it now—and getting at the truth. On the other hand, Benson might know exactly how to proceed. And there was still the man whom they knew as Mayhew...

And—Kerr sat up sharply in his seat, as this thought came to him—there was someone else they hadn't found yet. Mark Potter had been in the Daimler Penelope had followed before her accident.

Where was he now?

'I don't know,' admitted Gordon Craigie.

He was sitting opposite Kerr in one of the upstairs rooms of Common View. Miller was with them, and Trale, his leg bandaged, was sitting on a couch and scowling. Bob Carruthers, still a long way from recovering from the effects of the gas, was sharing the couch.

Craigie had arrived twenty minutes before, and learned what there was to learn. Every paper found in the house was on a table at his side. There was nothing helpful as far as was known, but he proposed to take them back to the office and study them more closely.

He had taken the news of Marlin's death coolly, but Kerr knew his man well enough to realise Craigie was relieved. Marlin, it was generally acknowledged, was the instigator of this game, and now he was gone there was a chance—if a slight one—of straightening the tangle out before it was too late.

So far, neither of the two men who had been caught while trying to escape from Common View had been persuaded to talk; but no-one as yet had tried to force them. Two others— the man in the hall and the man whose machine-gun Kerr had borrowed—were unconscious, the one likely to die without opening his lips, for the bullet had punctured his lung, and the other suffering from concussion. The Daimler in which Benson had escaped had been found abandoned five miles from the house.

Kerr broke a silence that had lasted for two minutes.

'How's the general situation?' he asked.

Craigie's mouth drooped.

'Not good. There was an ugly scene at the American Embassy this morning—some of it "inspired", of course. But too many American factories have closed. That's taken the working man's bread and butter, and he doesn't like it. We've told the White House,' he added, his face suddenly drawn, 'of Fenway's death. We couldn't keep it quiet any longer.'

'What did they say?'

'Little or nothing,' Craigie grimaced: 'But if it once gets into the American Press, there'll be no stopping them. Hopson has been more virulent than ever. Still, it's Benson we have to think about. What's our next step?'

Kerr smiled; Craigie had probably already planned the next move, but waited to hear what his agent's ideas were first.

'Search Potter's place more thoroughly,' Kerr suggested, 'and see what we can find about his friends—' He stopped suddenly. 'Good *God*!' he said softly, 'and we haven't seen it before. Craigie, we're blind! We don't want Potter's flat, and we don't want the Preston house—we want the factory!'

Craigie stared at him.

'But—'

'Oh, of course there are buts.' Kerr jumped up. 'I may be wrong. But ask yourself: Jeremy Potter must have been in this somewhere, or he wouldn't have been worth killing. His Secretary was in it. His brother may or may not be; that doesn't matter. But the only time Benson's used any number of men was in the raid at Preston when Davidson and I were there. The men disappeared completely. Where did they come

193

from? Somewhere in the Preston area, then Potter's factory— the mills! An ideal place for sheltering men!'

Kerr had crossed to the door and now stood holding it open impatiently. Craigie was silent for thirty seconds. Then:

'Will you fly up there?' he asked.

Kerr's expression changed and he smiled.

'Yes. From Heston. You'll telephone the Manchester people to keep the place watched? And a sharp look-out on the roads leading north for Benson or anyone like him! I wish,' he added, 'Tim and Wally could come, but they're at Dorchester—'

'They're on their way here,' said Craigie. 'Should arrive at any time. They telephoned me just after I heard from Miller.'

'Fine!' Kerr smiled. He felt completely fit again now. The prospect of further action had acted like a tonic on him. 'Are you coming?'

'No. I'm seeing Wishart this afternoon.'
'Dodo's out of it.' Kerr grinned his sympathy at the rueful Trale. 'So that makes four of us. Better see what Heston can do in the way of a six-seater cabin 'plane. How many telephones in this place?'

'One,' said Craigie, 'and I want it. But there are several next door.'

Kerr and Carruthers went next door, to the house of Mr. Reynoldson. The startled Town Clerk had hurried home after being telephoned about the damage done to his gardens. He took it well, however, and greeted the two men pleasantly enough.

'Your suspicions seem to have been justified, Mr.—er— Kerr. A dreadful business. Dreadful!'

'Beyond words,' agreed Kerr. 'I wonder—may I use your telephone?'

'By all means, by all means...'

Kerr had little trouble in fixing for the six-seater plane to be ready at Heston in half an hour. He thanked Reynoldson, who had been trying all day to remember where he had seen the man before (and realised it, two days later, when he saw an old paper showing Kerr after his Atlantic flight) and went out. As he reached the grounds of Common View, *via* the smashed mock-wall, he saw Davidson and Timothy Arran talking with the police on guard, and apparently having trouble in convincing them they were on business.

Kerr called out; the guard recognised him and let the two men pass.

'Next time,' said Timothy pugnaciously, 'you be a lot more civil, young feller-me-lad.' He winked, and the middle-aged policeman's annoyance melted in a chuckle.

Arran approached Kerr, his expression no longer cheerful.

'What happened to Pen?' he demanded.

'Craigie said something, but I didn't catch it.'

'She's doing fine,' Kerr reassured him.

'Have I time to pop over and see her? Where is she, by the way?'

'You haven't a spare minute,' said Kerr.

Timothy eyed him witheringly.

'Blast you,' he said. 'I'll get even one day. Where are we going?'

'Up north.'

'I'll be talking Lancashire before I've finished,' complained Timothy. 'And I suppose we have to fly with you?'

'It would be an idea,' said Kerr, equably, 'if you stopped playing the fool you are and practised looking intelligent.'

The appearance of Craigie at the door of Common View put an end to these pleasantries. He had arranged for the Preston police to keep the roads watched and the Potter factories surrounded, although at a good distance; they were to do nothing that might make anyone at the mills suspicious.

'You'll go up right away?' he asked.

They borrowed a police car for the drive to Heston, and en route, Timothy was avid for news. He asked questions, and learned that Kerr had given Marlin his quietus, that Kerr had played cricket with a Mills bomb, that Kerr had mooted the possible involvement of the Potter factories in this business, and suchlike, and generously informed him he was forgiven all his sins.

Of the four of them, only Kerr was thoroughly used to air travel. If it was not a novelty with the others, it was at least unusual to touch the two-fifty miles an hour that Kerr forced out of the Hawk Major in which they flew. Despite this, Timothy went so far as to say that the only safe place at the moment was in the air.

'Benson can't very well do any damage up here,'

'No,' said Kerr, slowly.

Timothy eyed him suspiciously.

'*Now* what's on your mind?'

'Thoughts,' Kerr told him. 'Just thoughts.'

Timothy relapsed into understanding silence, and enjoyed the panorama of summertime England. It was a sunny day, with no wind, and with little actual flying to do, Kerr stuck at the controls without thinking of his companions. There was an idea seeping through his head; not perhaps a reasonable one, but then it was little or no use to think normally now. He had to try to get one jump ahead of Benson.

What then would Benson do?

Kerr couldn't be sure; but the idea grew apace and he took a special air map from his pocket and studied it. He had an idea of the location of the Potter Mills, and he judged it would take them twenty minutes to get from the landing field to the factories. Twenty minutes was a long time.

His jaw was set as he pushed the joystick forward. The plane began to drop, and the landing-field loomed up before them. It was dusk, but they could see clearly enough. Timothy squinted over the side and reported three cars waiting:

'With any luck,' Kerr said drily, 'one of them should be ours.'

He was within twenty feet of the ground, and seemed to the others an interminable time settling the wheels. He had just touched down when there was a movement in one of the cars—by the driver who had been sitting until that moment apparently dozing—and in a moment, Kerr had opened the throttle. Timothy, who had been near the window, was thrown off his balance. Davidson opened his lips to protest— then saw the thing. Carruthers, whose experience with Kerr in the last few hours had shown him a thing or two, had his gun out first.

'Let 'em have it!' snapped Kerr.

As he spoke, the first stabs of flame from the machine-gun in the car-driver's hands split through the dusk. Bullets ripped along the side of the plane and into the wings. Carruthers blazed away at the car through an open door, although the wind almost knocked him off balance. Timothy was still sprawling on the floor and Davidson was already backing up with his gun, when the Hawk swooped upwards and out of range.

'We'll try and find the factories,' Kerr said, as though being machine-gunned was a perfectly normal event. 'It's damned dark now, but we might manage it.'

'Dead north from here,' Davidson offered.

'I know. A mile past the Larches, on the right of the

Lancaster Road,' said Kerr. 'One thing's certain; we've struck oil again.'

'Nothing's surer,' agreed Timothy Arran. 'Were you on the look-out for that, Bob?'

'I was.'

'Well, thanks,' said Tim drily, and Kerr and the others chuckled. But after that, they were silent—a silence that would have told anyone who knew these men that they were ready for the next attack.

Five minutes flying took them across Preston and above the Lancaster Road. The grey ribbon stretched out in front of them, straight for the most part and an excellent guide. They were flying low now, and all of them were looking down. They flew over the Larches—which Kerr identified—two minutes later, and within another sixty seconds they had sighted the long, low buildings on the right of the main road.

The Potter Cotton Mills...

'Now I wonder,' Timothy mused, 'if they'll be waiting for us there?'

'I hope to God,' Kerr said, 'that if they are, they don't start trouble in the place itself.'

The thought had a sobering effect, for all four men realised that there were several hundred men and women in the factory, probably none of them with any idea of the thing that might happen. If Benson was there and prepared to put up another fight, the casualties might be appalling.

The prospect of forcing the issue would have deterred most men. But Robert McMillan Kerr saw beyond the factory and the workers: saw the probability of war that would set the world alight. He had to take chances, even if it meant terror down here.

He put the nose of the plane towards the ground—and as he did so, saw the light on the roof of one of the buildings.

There were a dozen of these—long, low sheds—and the lights streaming from the windows of these was what they had seen for the past three minutes. But this other light was different...

Kerr's lips tightened as he saw the two figures scrambling on to the roof. He had already chosen his landing place, a small enough field but one he could manage, and he went for it quickly. As they flew over the roof, they could see the two men clearly; and even more clearly, they saw the stabs of flame shooting towards them, and felt the impact of bullets on the under-carriage.

'Here we go,' said Timothy Arran, tautly. 'Anyone for Hades?'

It was the only sound save the rattling of the machine-gun and the humming of the plane as they went down to force the final issue.

18

DISASTERS

The Hawk lost height smoothly, and Bob Kerr judged his distance to a nicety. The wheels hit the ground, bumped a little and then steadied. He shut off the engine and taxied to a standstill. Timothy Arran and Bob Carruthers were by the door, guns in hand, with Davidson at the other side in case of accidents. But the trouble would be more likely to come, they reckoned, from the building itself.

On the ground the Potter Cotton Mills seemed considerably larger than they had done from the air. Through the windows, the Department men could see men and girls working: the noise of aeroplane and machine-guns had not penetrated the hum of machinery in the factory itself.

They could not see the building where the machine-gunner had been stationed, but knew it could not be long before they were attacked; they didn't know how. Like every development in this game, they were up against the unknown all the time.

'One of us by the 'plane?' Davidson murmured, as they gazed about them through the grey dusk. 'No need,' said Kerr, briefly. 'I wish to heaven this thing had a radio. But wishing won't help. Split up, you fellows; one at each corner, as near as we can do it, and yell or shoot if you see anything suspicious. Craigie's message ought to have the police about here by now, and we'll have some help. Good luck!'

They split up. They saw the wisdom in Kerr's plan, although they realised that none of them would have a great chance if Benson or his men stumbled across him.

Where *was* Benson? What had happened to the gunmen on the roof? Where would the next attack start? These and a dozen other queries flashed through Bob Kerr's mind as he made his way towards the front of the factory. Here, the building was taller—the offices, he needed no telling—and lights came from nearly all the windows. Occasionally he heard the tapping of a typewriter. The silence grew. It seemed almost as if that machine-gun had been an illusion...

Craigie's instructions to the local police had been clear enough. They were to surround the factory at a fair distance, and stay there until they had further instructions. That meant Kerr had to get in touch with Preston headquarters or Craigie. He chose the headquarters as the way to get sharpest action, particularly as he might have to wait for the operator to put through a trunk call. Always supposing he could get to a telephone.

Benson seemed to have suspected he would come here. The one question that really wanted answering was: how many men had Benson primed, and where were they sheltering?

In the factory? The offices? The outbuildings?

Had he arrived without any interference, he would simply have gone to the office, telephoned the police to close in, then ordered the workers in the factory and offices alike to submit to interrogation: a big job, but not an impossible one.

Now, however—

Kerr didn't see the man hidden in the shadows of a clump of trees. But Benson spoke, and there was something vile in his voice.

'You think you're mighty smart, don't you, Kerr?'

For a moment, Kerr's mind stood still; he thanked the fates that his legs didn't. He jumped sideways as the gloom was split by the flame of a silenced revolver shot.

Benson was *here!* As the realisation flashed through his mind, he experienced a moment's exhilaration—even as he fired automatically in the direction of the flame. He didn't expect a hit, but he did mean to create a disturbance and could guess at the expression on Benson's face when the shot echoed loudly through the night. He had removed his own silencer, guessing gunfire would bring the police,

'You...!' swore Jacob Benson, and fired again.

Kerr was breathing very softly now, bending double as he ducked again. Benson seemed to be alone at the moment, but he couldn't be sure, and cursed the gloom—although in some ways it saved him; if he couldn't see Benson, Benson certainly could not see him. He could hear him breathing, and saw the flash of the third shot.

Then there was the sound of hurrying footsteps from two directions, and Davidson's voice came:

'All right, Kerr?'

'Interviewing Benson,' called Kerr, and jumped to one side. A bullet whipped into the tree where he had been standing; he could hear Benson's breath getting harsher and smiled grimly to himself as he cautioned: 'Steady all of you.'

A fifth shot stabbed the gloom, and he laughed aloud, He could guess how the sound jarred on Benson's ears.

'The end, my friend. You're going Marlin's way!'

'If I am,' Benson grated, and Kerr was convinced now that he was alone: 'I'm taking someone with me.'

Kerr fired towards the sound, but knew by the flash from Benson's gun that his shot had gone wide. He tried again, and Benson laughed uglily.

'But first I'm going to pump your stomach full of lead!' he taunted—and fired again, from several feet further to the right. 'How many men you got, Kerr?'

The stealthy movements of Arran, Davidson and Carruthers told him they were very near now. Benson was hemmed in—and he was between them and the wall. But— why was he talking?

Kerr had a sudden recollection of the way Mrs. Trentham had tried to gain time by stalling him: Benson was probably doing the same thing. There was the danger, too, of another gas attack: at any moment, Benson might throw one of those little phials...

'Three,' he replied. And Davidson, who heard him, gasped aloud at what seemed the madness of telling the truth: if he'd said a couple of dozen, he felt, Benson might have given up the fight.

But Kerr was seeing further than that. If Benson thought he had a chance of fighting through again, he might take it— and in doing so, take risks.

'Three, have you?' sneered Benson. 'Well, you won't have, for long!'

The tension grew; there was something at once ominous and sinister in Benson's words. He didn't seem to be boasting, and that probably meant he had something up his sleeve. *What?*

Kerr laughed again, and no one in the world would have believed that he was on tenterhooks, that his nerve was nearly breaking. The combined effect of the morning's ordeal, the affair at Wimbledon, the flight, the shooting and now this, had depleted his resources more than he knew; he had a job to prevent himself from getting hysterical.

'No, not for long,' he agreed. 'Another ten minutes, Benson, and I'll have a couple of hundred.'

'Will you!' Benson growled.

Crouching behind a small shrub, Kerr wondered whether he had succeeded. Would Benson act more quickly and rashly now, than he might have done? As he waited, tensed and anxious, Davidson was suddenly and silently at his side.

He had time to grunt: 'Keep low, man!' And then it happened.

One moment, they were in darkness and near-silence. The next, there was a mutter of voices, the rattle of chains, the creak of hinges—and the light.

It came from an enormous searchlight, which spread its powerful beam for hundreds of yards from the doorway near which Kerr was crouching. Davidson mumbled something as he ducked down, blinded by it. It was dazzling, overpowering— and paralysing, in its utter unexpectedness. They hardly heard Benson's triumphant:

'That's finished you, Kerr!'

But Kerr's senses were alive again in a flash. Hidden by the bushes as he was, he dropped to his stomach and, with a jerk at Wally's sleeve, rolled rapidly away. Wally followed a split-second later—just as the spot where they had been hiding was riddled by machine-gun fire.

Out of the direct range of the dreadful glare, Wally was still blinking dazedly. But Kerr was re-loading at speed. Outlined in the glow, he could see Benson, with two of his henchmen at his side. What he could not see, was that one of these was hefting the deadly tommy-gun. Then as Timothy Arran's voice shouted an anguished warning, he saw the vicious snout of it swivelling round towards him. So that just when a split-second could have spelt the end, he levelled his automatic and emptied it into the little group by the door. He saw the machine-gun waver towards the ground, then stop firing as the man went down. He saw Benson throw up his arms and heard him swear—foul, obscene oaths that rent the air. He saw the third man turn and flee into the factory. Then he leapt forward, aware of the shadowy figures of Carruthers and Arran approaching, Davidson in the rear.

It didn't seem possible that it had actually happened. *Benson* down; Marlin *and* Benson—finished!

Benson was writhing, his hands clutching at his stomach, his face distorted. And even in the comparative darkness behind the searchlight, Kerr could see one thing that explained many others: Benson's famous thick moustache was false. It was loose now, giving a grotesque effect to the appearance of the dying man.

'Kerr, you swine!' Benson mouthed. 'I knew you'd get me—I knew it all along. And Marlin. But I'll get you, Kerr, I'll rip your stinking insides out—'

Even as he spoke, one hand left his stomach and snatched at the sheath knife in his belt. But before the blade was bared, Kerr had his wrist; and Benson's strength was almost gone.

'Don't be a fool, Benson,' Kerr said, quietly.

'Get it off your mind before you go. Who's Mayhew? And where is he?'

Benson's snarl was his only answer.

'Talk!' said Kerr, urgently. 'It'll help you—and others.'

'Go—to—' began Benson. And then he stopped, and the expression in his eyes was maniacal. He started to laugh: high-pitched, ringing peals of insane laughter, the laughter of a man who knew he was dying and cared nothing for it. It was frightening and horrible.

'You'll find Mayhew!' he screeched. '*Maybe*! You wait till the arsenal goes up, and then look for him! You—'

He choked on the word: and his eyes suddenly glazed over as he gave one last, convulsive shudder: and lay still.

Twenty minutes later, Kerr was on the telephone to Craigie. He spoke briefly and concisely, yet Craigie knew he was talking under a tremendous strain.

'We got Benson. Dead. The police are in possession of the factory, now. Yes, it was used by Benson half the time. A dozen men have come in since—into the hands of the police. They were supposed to work here. Lived in the workers' quarters— a basement beneath the canteen. It's the headquarters all right. But, Craigie—'

'Yes?' The Chief of Department Z waited, as Kerr gave the news slowly, his own disappointment manifest.

'Not a paper anywhere. No clue to Mayhew, and only one hint to help us. Benson said: "Wait till the arsenal goes up." And that might be one of a dozen places.'

Craigie was silent for a moment, before he answered.

'Yes... Nothing else at all?'

'Nothing. The men won't talk. They swear they hadn't had their orders for today.'

'But Benson spoke as though the thing would happen?'

'Yes.' Kerr took a deep breath. 'I can't believe he'd bluff us when he was dying. Some mine's set at one arsenal or another— you'll just have to evacuate the lot. I'm damned sorry, Craigie—I've been trying for ten minutes to force some kind of information out of the swine here, but so far, not a word.'

'Don't worry, Kerr. You've warned us—that's bought us a bit of time: I'll have every arsenal neighbourhood cleared in the next hour,' Craigie promised. And wondered bleakly just how many men, women and children lived near even the smallest of them. Thousands, no doubt. And tens of thousands, at some of the others. 'Anything else to report?'

'No,' said Bob Kerr, wearily. 'I'm up against the same blank wall as before. Worse, if anything. Mayhew's a legend. Mark Potter's disappeared—he's our only real hope.'

'Don't forget, one of the officials at the factory might be in it,' Craigie suggested.

'Not very deeply,' Kerr said, 'but I'll remember.'

He replaced the receiver and turned away, his face dark, his bearing dejected. He'd found Marlin and he'd found Benson—and killed both men before they could talk. The realisation seemed to weigh on his soul. He told himself that if another disaster took a toll of human life, he couldn't face it. And deep down there was a consciousness that if he couldn't find the truth and show it to the world, the clash would come: the inferno no-one would be able to stop.

'Oh God!' he muttered 'Oh, my God!'

'Steady, old son.' Timothy Arran was looking white about the gills, and for once there was no facetiousness on the lips of Davidson and Carruthers. They, too, saw the dreadfulness of what might come. 'It isn't your fault. You've done your damnedest—'

'And thrown the chance away!' snapped Kerr.

'You will, if you let it get you down,' said Timothy quietly.

'I know,' Kerr straightened his shoulders. 'Get me a drink, someone?'

They were in the office of the managing director of the Potter Mills—the office of the late Jeremy—and an investigation of its cupboards revealed whisky and glasses. Kerr took half a tumbler and tossed it down his throat. The burning of it seemed to put new life in his veins, though he knew such a stimulant would not last long by itself. He wanted to act; God, how he wanted to act! And he couldn't. He didn't know where to start. Every possible line was gone. Even Penelope Smith had proved—as well as anyone could prove—her part was innocent. Why else should Benson have tried to smash her? There remained Mayhew, as much a mystery as ever. And Mark Potter, who seemed to have vanished off the face of the earth.

A blank wall—with an inferno on the other side of it.

'There's only one way,' David Wishart was telling Craigie, minutes later. 'And that is by wireless. And if we radio the arsenals and nearby towns and villages to evacuate, we'll have the country up in arms in a moment. Damn it, Halloway's back today with Cathie after a general tour of factories. No complaints were made.'

'I know,' said Craigie, 'but if you don't do it, you'll have a disaster compared with which Pockham was a pin-prick. You'll murder thousands, Wishart. That's what it amounts to.'

'Thousands—to save millions.'

'To prevent war, you mean? Do you think this thing—when it comes—can be kept quiet? Don't you think a reasoned appeal over the air to the people will keep them steadier than if the papers come out with the story of another disaster; a thousand times bigger than this one?'

'Well stop the papers printing it!'

'You can't stop leaflets being showered from the air!' snapped Craigie. 'You can't stop someone getting on the air from Germany—Italy—France—America—any country in the world. You can't keep news of an explosion quiet, these days.

It's impossible. Well—' Craigie turned away. 'It's up to you. I've done all I can.'

Wishart stared as the Chief of Department Z reached the door. The Premier's eyes held horror; his face was as gaunt as Craigie's now, his hair almost white. His hands were trembling too, and his voice was shaky as he spoke.

'Gordon—stop a minute. How—how do you want the message to go out?'

Craigie turned, and for the first time during that interview, he smiled gently.

'Good man, David!' he said, for he knew just what the decision was costing Wishart. 'Like this...'

It was twenty minutes later that the programmes at all British wireless stations were interrupted with the brief announcement: 'A message is to be broadcast to the nation by the Prime Minister in five minutes. Please stand by.'

During that five minutes, millions of people who had not heard the announcement were called into homes, theatres, cinemas—everywhere. The nation was agog. A message from Wishart, they thought, could mean only one thing...

Wishart's even voice, controlled by a strength of purpose he had not believed himself possessed of, came quietly into several million homes: grave, measured, and yet in a way reassuring.

'My broadcast tonight,' he opened, 'is a grave one, and urgent. It concerns in some measure the anxiety throughout the country at certain disturbances and disasters, and it is calculated to save life.' Wishart paused for a moment, and in those millions of homes there was a silence that could almost be felt. He went on slowly: The police and the Military have had orders to evacuate all towns and villages within a three-mile radius of those parts of the country which, it is believed, are in danger. The instigator of that danger—' Wishart's voice grew stronger now—'is not known, but the Government emphatically does not believe it to be the United States of America.'

Ministers and Members of Parliament who had not been informed in advance of this step, gasped as they criticised Wishart for singling out any one country for mention. 'Accommodation, of necessity temporary, will be found for all those who have been or will be ordered to vacate their homes, and stern measures will be taken against disobedience. That is the message of warning I have to broadcast, and I want you all to understand very clearly—particularly those of you who will suffer in any way through this emergency order—that it is *to save life.* For the rest—' Wishart's voice quavered a little now, although there was still a note in it that reminded those who had heard his speech in Parliament a few days earlier, of his unsuspected power—'I will say this to the people of Great Britain: We do not want war. We do not believe that any country is deliberately planning war against us. And I caution you all to patience; I plead with you, for that patience. That is all.'

The message was broadcast at five minutes past six on that March evening, and caused a bigger sensation than anything sent through the ether in the history of radio. Fast upon it, local broadcasts were made, and the evacuations were carried out in an astonishingly short space of time. Occasionally a protest was voiced, attempts to move heavy furniture and valuable possessions were made: but the police and the Military were adamant; men, women and children only, was the order; and thousands flocked from their homes to be marshalled into order with surprising docility. There had been a quality in Wishart's tone that had won their trust; had made them accept his claim of urgency as genuine.

Factories of all kinds were deserted, ships left lintended, aeroplanes stood in their hangars without guards or attendants. By half-past seven, the order had been carried out even more thoroughly than either Kerr or Craigie had even hoped for...

Half an hour later, all London rocked when the Thameside Arsenal was blown to smithereens. *H.M.S. Dukor* was blown into the air, the Kalshot naval base was razed to the ground, and up and down the country, large and small arsenals went up in searing, shattering explosions. And as the reports came in from the different centres, the tension at Whitehall grew. For Wishart and Craigie and the others knew only to well what this whole appalling record of disasters meant.

Great Britain's reserve of armaments and ammunition was practically non-existent!

19

KERR IS TALKATIVE

I t may have been the whisky, or perhaps simply his innate
inability to accept defeat, that gave Kerr new strength. At
all events for three hours after the death of Benson and his
men, he grilled officials and others of the Potter Cotton Mills.
But he learned nothing, and was finally convinced there was
nothing to be learned from them.

Twenty men—some English, some Continental but most
of them American—who had lived in the quarters beneath the
large canteen, had returned to meet Benson, as they had
thought, and instead found the police ready and waiting. Half
a dozen of them made a fight for freedom; none escaped. But
all of them maintained—even under pressure that made Kerr
hate himself—that they had come to the factory for instructions that evening. They had no idea what those instructions
might have been. It seemed the secret had died with Benson
and Marlin.

Kerr asked the questions. Few of the answers were satisfactory; most of the men, even though they knew Benson was
dead, were remarkably faithful to him. Kerr knew this type.

Each man he interrogated was a killer, who bought and sold life without conscience or compunction. They were certainly not the kind to remain faithful to an idea.

'So,' Kerr summed up—he and the others were still using Jeremy Potter's office—'they're afraid of trouble coming if they talk. They know Marlin and Benson are dead. So the someone else must be Mayhew.'

'Or Potter,' Timothy Arran offered.

'I wonder,' murmured Kerr, 'whether by any freak of chance, Potter and Mayhew are one and the same? It's useless to go by the fact that Jeremy Potter's servants pretended they didn't know him; they were Benson's men.'

'The women weren't.'

'As far as we know,' Kerr corrected.

'Then the butler, Oakwood, wasn't,' Davidson reminded him. 'And he claimed he'd seen Mayhew without recognising him.'

'Thick glasses, a moustache and a limp,' said Kerr, 'are more or less effective as a disguise. Oh, blast this business! I'm tired of repeating the names. Mayhew—Potter—Penelope—'

'Here, hang on!' protested Timothy.
'Oh, don't be a fool!' Kerr's temper was fraying. They're the only names we've got! And a fat lot of use they are to us. If I could only see what's *behind* it! Why should anyone want us to quarrel with the States? There has to be a motive—what the hell IS it? Who the hell is—'

He stopped suddenly and stared blankly at Wally Davidson, who wondered for a moment if the thing had finally gotten Kerr down. Wally was not to know that inspiration had dropped on Kerr from the skies: *two* motives at once. *Two motives to make one...*

He moved as he was wont to move, and Timothy Arran

jumped away from the desk on which he was lounging as Kerr grabbed the 'phone and called Whitehall 55055.

'Kerr,' he said. 'Craigie—who's the biggest *private* armaments manufacturer in England to-day?'

Craigie, puzzled and tired, frowned at the other end of the line.

'Dickers-Leestrong, of course.'

'Of course. Find out who holds most of their shares, directors and/or otherwise. Remember, Marlin brought and sold armament shares? See who he did most work for. You might find—just *might*—that Wishart and other members of the Government dealt in those shares, some time or other. Find anyone who stopped buying and started selling about the same time that *Mayhew* started buying.'

'Good God!' said Craigie, who rarely blasphemed.

'And think on this,' Kerr spoke tensely, but every word reached the men in the room as well as Craigie. 'This shouting about the States is *eyewash*. *Eyewash*, Craigie. Nobody but a pack of born fools would ever have thought twice about it. Of course we're not going to fight America! But we're so damned busy thinking we might, that we've forgotten the folk who might fight us.'

'There isn't another country strong enough,' Craigie interrupted: 'They're too busy with internal affairs.'

'Internal—and other things,' said Bob Kerr. 'Think of the mid-European Entente. Bounded on all sides. Agitation for colonies. Wanting mandated territories back—bellowing for them! We won't let 'em have them and the League won't. So—damn it, Craigie, you *can* see?'

'Go on,' said Gordon Craigie, very softly.

'So they pay Benson and Marlin to raise the Anglo-American scare. They keep us busy—and they've done it damned well. And then they get at our armaments. Supposing the

Entente start a flare-up to take the mandated territories—how could we stop it, right now?'

'We'd find it difficult,' Craigie agreed, drily. Inwardly he was wondering whether Kerr was talking nonsense, or whether at last things were taking shape. For he knew that until the American scare, the one thing that might have caused trouble had been the natural desire of the mid-European Entente for a share of the mandated territories and colonies. And he knew that if the Entente started trouble, Italy (again) and Germany for the first time would probably join them. A common cause, for both democratic and dictator-ridden countries. Yes... It seemed to be making some sort of sense, at long last.

'*Difficult!*' Kerr echoed, and swore eloquently. 'We've been kept so busy we haven't had time to think what the European countries are up to. Now they've got us. The Entente will demand certain territories; and soon Hitler and Mussolini will start bellowing, too. And if we say they can't have them, they'll turn nasty. They'll invite us to stop them. *And we haven't the arms, Craigie—we couldn't do it!*'

'You know, Kerr,' said Craigie quietly. 'If you're anywhere near right, they can start when they like.'

'Wait a minute,' Kerr told him. The idea that had dropped on him seemed like manna from the skies; he had to get it out: 'With England and America at loggerheads, the one country that might help us is off the books. Right? Get rid of the loggerheads, let the U.S. and Britain show a united opposition, and the Entente's plan is scotched—because America's got arms and to spare, right?'

'Right.'

'Then all we've got to do,' Kerr wound up cheerfully, 'is to show America that the whole thing—from the *Akren* onwards —has been a campaign to blind both countries to the truth. It isn't a question of actual *fighting*; it's only a question of being able to say: 'We're too strong for you! Isn't it?'

Craigie's dry grin came and went. Solemnly, he conceded: 'It looks like it. Er—how are we going to show America who's behind it? You haven't found Mayhew?'

'Not yet,' said Kerr, 'but I daresay we will. You'll have those gentry who have trafficked in arms shares and such looked after?'

'I'll have them watched.'

'Good!' Kerr's cheerfulness was beginning to puzzle the other Z men. 'See if you can find one of them with access to all the Government-owned and controlled arsenals. How many places met trouble to-night?'

'About a dozen.'

'You see? Benson was clever and Marlin was clever, but neither of them could have located a *dozen* strongly-guarded places like that. *And* deposit time-bombs to start the damage. Whoever gave them the information *knows* it from A to Z. Look for someone closer to Whitehall, Craigie, and your troubles will be over.'

Gordon Craigie's voice was bleak. 'I shouldn't be surprised,' he said slowly, 'if you're right. I think I see what you mean.'

'I thought you would,' said Kerr. 'All you want is a man who's going to make two or three million profit out of re-fitting us with armaments, whose factories are going to start working overtime and who can't account for his movements on the days Mayhew was seen about. Someone with Fascist convictions, you can be pretty sure.'

'Perhaps we'll know by the time you get here,' said Craigie, drily. 'Goodbye.'

Robert McMillan Kerr turned from the telephone and

regarded Carruthers, Davidson and Timothy Arran. All were looking dazed.

'Who the hell are you driving at?' asked Timothy.

'You ought to know.' Kerr's unexpected smile lingered longer than usual. 'You certainly should know.'

'What's on that piece of paper?' Davidson demanded.

'What, this?' Kerr unscrewed the sheet he had been glancing at when the idea had flashed across his mind. 'It's a letter from the Potter Company's London office—or Mark Potter—to the Lancashire management. About an export order for cotton fabric to Europe, I think.'

Davidson, suspicious, read it for himself, but gained nothing from it. 'You think we've run to the end of it, then?' he asked, still baffled.

'I do,' said Kerr, 'but I want to get to London, pronto. I wonder if they carry petrol here?'

'I suppose,' said Timothy, witheringly, 'you *will* tell us all about it in the air?'

'You've seen just as much as I have,' Kerr baited him, then chuckled. 'Still, it won't hurt you to know one more thing: Mark Potter's dead.'

'*Dead!*'

'Nothing's surer. Tim, who did we find at Wimbledon?'

'Marlin and Benson and some hoodlums—but what's that got to do with it?'

'Who ought to have been at Wimbledon, according to Penelope?'

'Now look here,' began Timothy irritably, 'you've played on that girl long enough, old son.'

'Wait a minute,' interrupted Davidson. '*Mark Potter.* You reckon he's one of the men who was killed there? One of the gunmen?'

Kerr shook his head. 'Describe Benson,' he invited—and headed for the door.

In the minds of all three there sprang a picture of a thick-set florid-faced man of perhaps fifty, with a heavy black moustache and a harshly unpleasant voice...

From the doorway, Kerr grinned.

'Think of Mark Potter,' he said, and went out.

By the time the Hawk was re-fuelled, Mark Potter's body had been identified beyond all doubt. But the three Department men were still dazed as they started back for London.

It all seemed so obvious, now. Benson had never been seen without that heavy moustache, and when Penelope had seen her uncle in the car going towards Wimbledon, and there had been no sign of him there, but ample evidence of Marlin and Benson—the thing should have struck them then. Or those of them, Timothy thought thankfully, who had been on the job at the time; thank heavens he hadn't been. Then there was the ease with which Mark Potter could ensure refuge for the gunmen at the factory: Jeremy had probably discovered it and threatened disclosure, and the woman Trentham warned his brother. No stranger had been seen to enter the house, that day: Mark Potter had a key and could come and go as he liked. Again 'Benson' had entered The Larches by key. And 'Benson' must have known the lay-out of the factory thoroughly. Oh, it was maddeningly obvious, now!

Timothy thought of the shock Penelope would have, and scowled; thought of Penelope in other circumstances, and smiled. He closed his eyes and his thoughts were very pleasant.

* * *

David Wishart refused to believe what Craigie had to tell him. But as he examined the evidence, he slowly came to see the truth. And Craigie realised that the truth was in fact a bigger blow to Wishart than the thought of war with America itself.

'The important thing now,' Craigie emphasised, 'is to convince America. I've an idea of how to do it, but I'm by no means sure you'll like it. I hope you will.'

'If we can convince them,' Wishart said, 'anything is worth trying. We've got to get them friendly. We *must*.'

'Good,' said Gordon Craigie. 'Well, here it is...'

Wishart listened; at the end of five minutes he nodded. He was not smiling; he felt he would never be able to smile again, although Craigie knew better.

'About mid-day here, is a good time,' Craigie wound up.

'To-morrow?'

'My dear David,' Craigie protested, 'This is urgent! To-day. In a couple of hours' time.'

'But I've got to call them together...'

'Call all you can,' advised Craigie.

In this nightmare business, so many unprecedented things had happened that there were times when Wishart felt guilty of breaking Constitutional rules as well as traditional ones. Even when he had agreed to follow Craigie's suggestion, there was still approval to be obtained from a higher source.

It was granted without question, and Wishart felt more cheerful as he returned to Downing Street and joined with his secretary in calling those members of the Cabinet who were in London. In the next hour, too, certain people who had visited Downing Street before, were there in greater numbers.

Craigie was the last to arrive, with Robert McMillan Kerr, who had never seen more than two of the assembled company together in his life before, but was neither impressed nor over-awed. He knew Halloway, of course, and Yelding, the Air Minister; they were good friends, and shook hands warmly. Lee-Knight recognised him and waved; Sir James Cathie stared at him critically and confided to his neighbour that it was coming to something, when policemen could be brought into the Cabinet Room. As Kerr caught the aside and chuckled, Cathie's stare grew frigid, and his dislike crystallised.

'Now, gentlemen!' The Prime Minister eyed each man in turn. 'We have neither the time nor the need to worry about preliminaries this morning. One of the chief reasons I have called you here at such short notice is to let you hear some—er —remarkable theories elucidated by Mr. Kerr, who will need no introduction and who is, as you know, an Intelligence Department agent. May I say first, that it was thanks to Mr. Kerr's warning that the arsenals and surrounds were evacuated last night, in consequence of which, it can safely be claimed, at least ten thousand lives were saved. I might add that it is his opinion that there is little or no immediate danger of war with America. Mr. Kerr?'

Kerr stood up and looked about him slowly. He could change the *tempo* of this meeting, and he needed no telling that he would be received reasonably and favourably. The evacuation order had earned him that. He smiled and started...

It took him ten minutes to elaborate the theory he had outlined to Craigie, the previous night. He worked up to his point slowly, first stressing the obvious interest of countries without colonies. 'The only sound reason,' he emphasised, 'for any country to risk war today, is for the winning of new territory—new guaranteed markets, new guaranteed sources of supply, new commercial or politically strategic bases. In a word, gentlemen: colonies. Someone—some body of men is prepared to risk war with us. I am going to submit that the motive is envy of our territories, mandated and otherwise.'

'No evidence,' interrupted Cathie, belligerently.

'None at all,' agreed Kerr, with an easy smile. 'But before we discuss evidence, I want to tell you of several interesting discoveries—all made in the course of investigations into the various disasters which culminated in last night's chaos.'

He talked of the attack at Wimbledon and the death of Marlin. He pointed out the likelihood that whoever was backing Marlin was a client of his in the normal way. He switched over to the dual-personality of Jacob Benson and Mark Potter, elaborating it so that even Cathie had all the evidence he wanted. He touched on Mayhew—so far completely unknown—and he began to prove, slowly and convincingly, the obvious interest behind the upheavals.

'Someone in England,' he said, 'is prepared to take the abnormal risks involved in securing war, *for money!* No one with ample resources would do it; the risks would be too great. Therefore it is someone whose resources are low. Gregory Marlin, naturally, would know which client, interested largely in the manufacture of armaments, would be prepared to give him information about the location of the more important arsenals *and* take an active part in their destruction.'

'Are you seriously suggesting,' protested Yelding, 'that anyone would start these outrages simply to obtain the orders for new supplies?'

'Partly,' said Kerr. 'For that sole purpose, no. But with an additional bribe for Marlin—representing certain foreign interests, whose main object is to weaken Great Britain's armed strength—yes. It would work like this: Marlin would be approached by those interested, and he would know of a man whose resources were low—*and* who was in a position to help him—who would benefit from a demand for armaments.'

'I can't believe it,' said Yelding, bluntly.

'No.' Bob Kerr flashed that unbelievably engaging grin. 'But *someone* has tried to inflame opinion here and in America. The circumstances are clearer, now. Mark Potter and Marlin definitely did so; the proof is ample. Now we have that proof, I think we can safely rely on more amicable relations between this country and America, with the resultant safeguards these can ensure. For the rest: someone *did* go on board the *Dukor*, *did* visit the various arsenals during the past two or three days and deposit time-bombs. Someone *has* been to Kalshot and arranged for the blow-up there. Someone whose presence at all those places, either publicly or privately, would not be queried. Someone, gentlemen, *now in this room!'*

Robert McMillan Kerr turned towards David Wishart, it seemed in accusation.

The silence in the room was electric. All eyes were, on Wishart, now, as shocked incredulity gave way to wonder. All of them realised that Wishart *had* lost heavily in his monetary transactions, *had* been a prominent client of Gregory Marlin's —and had continually recommended Marlin to other members of the Cabinet, as well as friends.

Wishart, who had disappeared from time to time in the past few days, ostensibly on business with Craigie...

Wishart!

'I think I should add,' said Bob Kerr, calmly, 'that I first suspected who was with Marlin and 'Benson' in this business when I discovered who was on the Board of the Potter Cotton Mills. I was blinded for a while because the Potter connection seemed so different from what it was.' He eyed Wishart steadily, and every other eye was turned on the Prime Minister's pale face; Wishart looked as though he could not stand the strain a moment longer. 'Well, Mr. Wishart?'

'I cannot convince myself,'—Wishart's voice trembled as he spoke—that your suspicions are well-founded, Mr. Kerr.'

'No?' said Kerr, drily. 'It took me a long time, too.' He surveyed the assembled company again, from Lee-Knight to Yelding: from Halloway to Cathie—who seemed struck dumb.

'Whoever it was,' he said, 'also appeared from time to time as Mr. Mayhew. He was adequately disguised. He used—these.' From a small packet he produced a pair of thick, horn-rimmed glasses, a wig of dark hair and a moustache to match. 'We traced Mayhew to an hotel in Bays-water,' he went on, 'and the manager assures me these effects are similar to those affected by Mayhew. They were found...'

The thing happened in a flash. Kerr could have prevented it, but had no desire to: there was only one satisfactory way for this to end. He saw Sir Kenneth Halloway leap from his seat, saw him snatch the revolver from his pocket. Yelding made an ineffectual, if plucky effort to stop him, but the bullet went through Halloway's forehead—and Kerr continued even as the man slumped down.

'They were found,' he said quietly, 'in Sir Kenneth Halloway's rooms at the Carilon Club, together with ample evidence to substantiate the story. And I think this evidence should be read out now, gentlemen—for America and the world is listening to this meeting, *over the air.*'

20

CONGRATULATIONS TO
AND FROM

I t had been intended primarily that the United States should hear the broadcast from Downing Street, but of necessity the rest of the world listened, and took startled note. In America, naturally, the effect was greatest; and like many examples of intense mass-feeling, the communal outcry against Great Britain swung round to a laudatory song of fellowship. Those sections of the Press that had been strongest against England were now out-doing each other in her praise.

The unprecedented step of broadcasting a Cabinet Meeting was generally conceded a master-stroke of diplomacy, impossible to combat. The tension of the meeting and the shot with which Halloway had killed himself had registered throughout the world, and obviously there was no question of the genuineness of the declaration. Even Big Bill Hopson was reported to have said that there was something in the spirit of those little islands, after all. The President telephoned London, congratulating Wishart on the way in which the threatened trouble had been averted, and promising to make sure the American end of the organisation was rounded up. 'Always assuming,' the President said, 'we can find them. Perhaps you'll have to send your men over, Wishart.'

Wishart smiled. That was as high a compliment as any man could have paid, and he told himself that Craigie deserved to hear it.

Craigie did, and he also heard later that Northway, shocked and hopeless in the face of the utter extermination of the English organisation, had finally let slip enough for its American counterpart to be rounded up.

With the filing of that American despatch, there was little left to do. The thing was history now—if, for the most part, history that would never be officially recorded. Puffing contentedly at his meerschaum, the Chief of Department Z smiled as he began to write his final report.

'There are times,' said Gordon Craigie to David Wishart and a Certain Personage, 'when some operations of Secret Service work have to be made public, and I don't think Kerr was far wrong in asking for that discussion to be broadcast. There's no question of the success of its reception in America; it has entirely changed the outlook of the States with regard to this country, and has raised a storm of protest in all the democratic nations. Any effort by the mid-European Entente to cause trouble can only fail, because of the united front against them.'

'Very different,' said the Personage, 'from what could have happened had we been suspected of deliberately picking a quarrel with—well, with any other country. Keep me in close touch with developments, Prime Minister, won't you?'

The Rt. Hon. David Wishart promised that he would.

Craigie left with him for the office of Department Z where Kerr was waiting. He greeted them cheerfully:

'I've been on the telephone since you left,' he added, to Craigie. 'The reports from America and the Continent are excellent. The Entente disclaims any part in the affair—I suppose it is only politic to accept that disclaimer?'

He sounded faintly wistful, and Craigie smiled drily.

'It certainly is.'

'And we certainly shall,' said Wishart, firmly. 'We've no proof to the contrary anyhow.'

Kerr cocked a humorous eyebrow.

'Haven't we? I'll take the chance of disagreeing with you, sir. There was a file of papers in the offices of the Potter Mills, concerning orders with the mid-European Entente. A cypher expert is working on them now, and I think you'll find they represent the—er—business arrangements between Marlin, Potter and the Entente.'

Wishart stared.

'Why should you suppose them to concern anything but normal business dealings?'

'Because the Entente put an embargo on imported cottons and fabrics, twelve months ago,' explained Kerr. 'I found a letter at the Potter offices, purporting to deal with orders for materials I knew to be forbidden, and the rest of the correspondence has been found since. Still,' he grinned engagingly again: 'I suppose it *is* the wise thing, to accept the disclaimer?'

And this time, Wishart—nodding firm agreement—returned his smile.

The broadcasting of that Cabinet meeting to the world evoked a universal call for peace. Great Britain, certainly, would not refuse to answer it.

'So it's over.' Wishart shook his head, almost unbelieving

still. Thank God. Although—I still can't think of Halloway without feeling—well—'

'I know,' said Kerr, slowly. 'The devil. Everyone thought—certainly, I did—that he had sold out all his interests in the munitions field. It was only much later that it struck me as queer that the mysterious Mayhew popped up in Marlin's records at about the same time—Halloway's way of hanging on to most of his interests, of course.' He shook his head, baffled by the behaviour of the man. 'Remember how he was always yelling for heavier armaments? Ostensibly for our defence—actually, for quicker profits! Money-mad—literally. I mean it: he can hardly have been sane, can he?'

'He couldn't have been,' said Wishart, bleakly. 'The utter callousness of it all—!'

Craigie nodded grimly: 'Yes indeed. For one thing, he knew Mrs. Trentham was a fanatical Communist—so he first got her dependent on him for drugs, then placed her with Jeremy Potter, where she was able to keep all the records for the campaign.'

'And like a lot of other people,' Kerr suggested, 'she was prepared to commit any atrocity on paper, but when Mark Potter actually killed his brother, she broke down?'

'I'm told,' Craigie said flatly, 'that she's been inoculated with a serum that will eventually unhinge her.'

The other two grimaced their distaste, then Wishart asked: 'What of the man in America—Northway?'

Kerr shrugged. 'Communist, English-born—just the combination Marlin wanted to cause the agitation in the States. By the way, what's happened to him, Craigie?'

'He died,' Craigie said dourly. 'They called it heart failure.'

There was silence for a little, each man thinking of the horror that had passed—and the greater horror so narrowly averted.

'What first made you think of Halloway?' Wishart asked at last.

'The use of his car for the bomb-throwing at Downing Street,' Kerr answered. 'Of course that was only an idea, but I worked on it. And then he told me his commissions with Marlin had practically stopped, but that he knew him well. Then, he'd been associated with the Potters—and when I learned that at one time, he'd been Mrs. Trentham's employer —well, it all seemed too much for coincidence.' He smiled wryly. 'Nasty business, all round; but I suppose it might have been worse.' Rising, he looked at his chief. 'Do you want me any more, Craigie?'

'I shall,' Craigie replied drily, and Kerr grinned.

'I can have a couple of weeks off, I hope?'

'You never know,' said Craigie, returning the grin.

He shook hands, and Wishart followed suit. The expression in the latter's eyes said more than words could have done, and Bob Kerr was still smiling his pleasure as he hailed a taxi to take him to the Carilon Club. There he found, as he had expected, Timothy Arran, Wally Davidson, Bob Carruthers, a still-limping Dodo Trale, young Beaumont—and, unexpectedly, a somewhat tired but unquenchably cheerful person by the name of Tobias Arran. Toby, released from hospital for the celebration, announced that if he'd been on the job all along he would have cleared it up in a week. Magnanimously, they allowed him to stay...

They celebrated in the traditional Department fashion, but Kerr noticed that Timothy Arran was fidgety.

'Tired, Tim?' he asked.

'To tell you the truth,' said Timothy, 'I've a date. Pen's out of hospital to-day, following Toby's lead, and I'm going to collect her. I—er—she said she'd rather like to see you.'

'*Did* she!' chuckled Bob Kerr. 'She must have altered her

opinion. All right, let's leave these lads to their beer-swilling and get along. I'd rather like to see Penelope myself.'

'To apologise, I hope,' said Timothy.

'What for?'

'Your base suspicions, you lout.'

'I'll tell you what.' Kerr rested a hand on Timothy's arm: 'If I've apologised to her within the next two hours, I'll be your best man.'

'You be quiet,' said Timothy, uneasily. They were at the door by then, and he added in a stage-whisper: 'They're all fighting for the job.'

The noise that came from the beer-drinking gentlemen was effectively dramatic, but hardly polite. Timothy grinned and waved his goodbyes, then as he followed Kerr out, demanded: 'And what do you mean, blast you, by two hours' time? You'll apologise the minute you see Pen, or I'll know the reason why!'

'Exactly,' murmured Kerr.

'You're an obstinate cuss,' said Timothy, but without rancour: for him the world was fair that morning.

They reached the Wimbledon hospital in good time, and Penelope, looking very much better despite her bandaged head, shook hands warmly with Bob Kerr and smiled at Timothy. Timothy bridled immediately.

'I've told him,' he said, 'that you demanded an apology, and—'

He stopped; Kerr was eyeing Penelope oddly and Penelope was smiling back at him. Timothy had an unpleasant feeling in his mind that he might have taken Penelope too much for granted. Damn it, Kerr was a sight better catch for any girl. He was a ruddy fool, and deserved all he got. He was almost tempted to claim another appointment, but conquered the impulse.

'Penelope,' Bob Kerr was saying quietly—and to Timothy astonishingly: 'why didn't you join your aunt in Cannes?'

Penelope was smiling; Timothy waited, baffled, for her answer. When it came, it was an evasion.

'Can't you guess?'

'I probably can,' said Kerr. 'I'm quite an imaginative fellow, at times. I've an idea you believed Jeremy Potter was extremely anxious to get you away from England because trouble of some kind was brewing. That you weren't happy about it, and when you slept on Tim and Toby's spot of bother, you decided to come back. That you suspected Mark Potter was the mysterious Benson, and after you'd spent a week with your aunt, you decided to tack yourself on to him and see what you could find. In fact,' Bob Kerr said, no longer smiling, 'I believe that if you hadn't spotted him in that Daimler and gone after him we'd have been little nearer the solution, now.'

'You certainly have an imagination,' Penelope smiled.

'Timothy Arran,' said Bob Kerr, irrelevantly, 'you don't deserve her, but all the luck in the world, you two.' He planted a chaste kiss on Penelope's cheek. 'I want to look in on our friends at the Wimbledon Station. But you should be all right with our Tim. He's really quite a fellow when you know him.'

ABOUT THE AUTHOR

John Creasey, born in 1908, was a paramount English crime and science fiction writer who used myriad pseudonyms for more than six hundred novels. He founded the UK Crime Writers' Association in 1953. In 1962, his book *Gideon's Fire* received the Edgar Award for Best Novel from the Mystery Writers of America. Many of the characters featured in Creasey's titles became popular, including George Gideon of Scotland Yard, who was the basis for a subsequent television series and film. Creasey died in Salisbury, UK, in 1973.

DEPARTMENT Z

FROM OPEN ROAD MEDIA

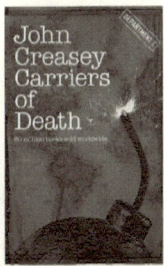

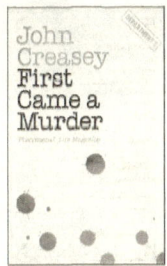

OPEN ROAD
INTEGRATED MEDIA

Find a full list of our authors and
titles at www.openroadmedia.com

FOLLOW US
@OpenRoadMedia

www.ingramcontent.com/pod-product-compliance
Lightning Source LLC
Chambersburg PA
CBHW020600030726
47497CB00007B/2018